VENTRILOQUISM

GUESS WHO'S TALKING?

VENTRILOQUISM

GUESS WHO'S TALKING?

Don Gaylord Bryan and Noseworthy

To order additional copies of this book, contact:
Xlibris
1-888-795-4274
www.Xlibris.com
Orders@Xlibris.com
771988

To
Federica

[signature]

Nswy: Hey, DB. I notice when you are lying, your
lips move, which is most of the time.
DB: I would appreciate it if you would keep
your mouth closed while I am talking.
Nswy: Why should I? You don't keep **your**
mouth closed when I'm talking!

Contents

Introduction to Don Bryan

Ventriloquist

Don Bryan is widely acclaimed as one of the world's top ventriloquists who have been delighting audiences for over thirty-five years. He is recognized as a creator of hand-carved, original, professional-quality puppet characters.

He was born in Newport, Wales, in 1941. Don now makes his home with his family in North Vancouver, British Columbia, Canada. He began learning the craft of ventriloquism at the age of nine years old. Inspired by his heroes of the time, Edgar Bergen and Paul Winchell, he began performing for friends and schoolmates in the '50s. One of his earliest triumphs as an aspiring performer came when he his sidekick, Clarence, made a hit at the Nuffield Centre in London, England, the armed-services showcase theatre. As a result, that show was given rave reviews in 1965 by the iconic theatrical newspaper the *Stage*. He then embarked on a tour of United Services Organizations bases throughout Europe. That early success inspired Don to continue working on his dream career as a professional working ventriloquist. Today he is known as one of the top ranking professionals in North America. In addition, he is recognized as one of the foremost creators of hand-carved, high-quality ventriloquist's puppets.

A couple of biker dudes during a promotion for HOG
(Harley Owners Group, rally event).

This is a bizarre shot of me with Clarence in 1966 when I worked for a tobacco company. They had me employed as a promotor of their products to the point of ridiculous. I didn't even smoke; neither did Clarence, just for the record. Could you imagine this kind of promotion today? They had me touring Safeway stores, malls, and bowling alleys, hyping their cigarettes. How the world has changed.

This book has been a long time in the making. Along with the course on the art of ventriloquism, I have compiled a short history on ventriloquism, the performers who have over the years influenced me, and my development as a professional.

The beginning for me was over sixty years ago. When I was nine years old, I was fascinated with the craft and all its mysteries, in particular the creation of the puppetry, their construction, the character's development, and animation mechanics. Still to this day, this fascination keeps me working to perfect my technique and craft.

I have included a number of photos of my puppet characters and some background. How did I come to the realization that it is now time to share some of my experience and knowledge of this craft? I want to encourage would-be ventriloquists, young and old, to get involved and learn the craft of "voice throwing" and, in particular, share what I have learned as a performer and figure builder. I will teach you the vocal techniques of ventriloquism, the basics that most anyone can learn with perseverance and dedication. You will learn how to amuse and even amaze your audience and skeptics with your skill within a surprisingly short time. Most ventriloquists today, at least at the professional level, began very young. That helps. The more years, along with experience, the better you will become. Having said that, however, I can tell you that within a few months, you will develop the ability to create the illusion and make believe that your character—puppet—is a personality entirely separate from yours. How much fun is that? You can often get away with humor and smart remarks, typical of this duo combination of you, the straight man, and the puppet the comedian, leaving your audience quite impressed if not amazed at your skill. The key to this success is your perfection of the basic techniques: lip control, your vocal transformation of the puppet voice, and animation of your vent figure (*vent* is a short term for ventriloquist).

The course I have laid out in this book will give you the tools to get started, beginning with simple vocal exercises and some breathing techniques. You will learn how to pronounce difficult words without using your lips and practice exercises that you can work on almost any time, almost anywhere. It is a good idea to not be caught talking to yourself in a public place, at least not without a puppet or a mobile phone. You might look a bit odd as well. Having said that, how often have we seen people talking on their telephones using a small wireless microphone, seemingly talking to an imaginary person? This vision has become accepted as the norm these days with mobile phones, but without the phone prop or a puppet, you may draw some odd looks. Just saying.

The really cool thing is you can use your ventriloquism to impress and surprise people by making it appear different inanimate objects are talking. A friend of mine, a very accomplished vent, made it appear his watch was talking. It was truly amazing and very effective. His watch actually was a talking watch, designed for people with visual impairments, so after demonstrating that function built into the watch, he continued on in his own "watch" voice with further comments and answered questions. It was very effective and funny and fooled the audience completely. The thing is he was able to imitate the watch voice so well that you actually believed the watch was talking, even though it was him. It was so much fun, he even had me thinking the watch was listening. This little trick can be learned using the techniques I have outlined in this book.

My first carved Clarence
character, looks about 1954.

This was shot a couple of years
later with the same character.

Bird Reynolds, the ever hungry vulture—this creation was
from an inspiration after a trip to Las Vegas in 1981.

I was aware of a large number of vulture cards and desert scenes with these bizarre birds. I thought it would be a neat idea to create my own version of a vulture, and this is how he turned out. It has a large wood-carved head and soft wire-framed body. He is a very impressive visual puppet that did well for me over the years. menacing but cute at the same time. "Patience, my butt. I'm going to kill something!"

Chapter One

The Family's Early
Years — 1952

We lived in an old two-and-half-storied home on Fourteenth Street in Vancouver, British Columbia. Our family of four had immigrated to Vancouver from London, England, in 1947. After moving around the province for a few years, following my father's business schemes, eventually, we settled in a leafy old neighbourhood close to downtown. I was eleven years old, attending school at Cecil Rhodes Elementary. I had a paper route and was not able to break even. It seemed I was always short somewhere in my paper-route accounts. I think I was being swindled by the paper, and the money was so small, it hardly was worth the effort, even if I was not losing money.

Small as the money was, for me, it was just a way and means of acquiring the materials I needed for my many projects. I was always building something, toys of my own imagination. I was fascinated with the unusual and continuously making some sort of new thing, whatever was my latest interest of the week. My parents were very liberal and encouraged me to pursue my many projects, puppets and ventriloquism being one of my interests. My father was an actor on the London stage, but in Vancouver, just after the war, there was no work for him in his profession. He was also an artist and painted many canvases when he wasn't out on a road trip but never made much money selling his artwork. Dad, Gaylord Sydney Bryan, took on what he could find from selling pots and pans, dishes, and vacuum cleaners. Those were lean years for the Bryan family. My mom worked too in a ladies' fashion house, selling women's clothes to help with the monthly bills. Both my parents were artistic and creative people. Unfortunately, they never got a break as artists. Somehow, between the two of them, they managed a decent middle-class income.

In those years before television, the Motorola radio was our entertainment centre. Sunday evenings were the roast-beef dinners, very traditional English fare. Often friends would drop in and stay for dinner. My friends knew what a great cook my mother was, and they would just happen around the house at dinner and inevitably would be asked to stay. My mother was very generous and liked having people drop in, not quite so with my father; he was a bit more conservative and liked to be without house guests, at least on weekends. He always complained that we couldn't afford to feed other people.

Sunday dinners were always accompanied with radio shows. We would put up a small table in the living room near the radio and listen to our favourite shows. Mine was, of course, the *Charlie McCarthy Show*, with Edgar Bergen and Charlie McCarthy. The program was very popular in those postwar years.

These shows were my introduction to ventriloquism. To begin with, I wasn't aware that the show was about a ventriloquist and his puppets. They would always have famous people as guests on the program performing radio plays with their famous guest stars along with their regular characters of the show. This was a magical time for me, enjoying the humour and stories that Bergen would go through with Charlie and Mortimer. Once I found out what the show was—about puppets and the ventriloquist—I had to find out more. I looked up Bergen in the encyclopedia, and there was the picture of Bergen and McCarthy. That just started my imagination going. Luckily, in the school library, there was a book on ventriloquists, an old English publication that had photos of puppets and lots of information. I devoured that. I kept it for months before I returned it, but I wanted to find out more about the fascinating craft, especially the puppets. I so wanted a ventriloquist's dummy.It wasn't long after this that our neighbour, a widow across the street, had a brand new television. This was around 1956. She invited me and my sister over on Sundays to watch shows, and that was when I discovered Paul Winchell and his sidekick, Jerry Mahoney. He was brilliant! His characters had articulated arms and seemingly sat alone, talking with animated bodies. The shows were groundbreaking at the time, with so many innovations with puppet animation. This really got me hooked on the whole idea of somehow getting my hands on a puppet.

That Christmas, my father bought me a Jerry Mahoney figure from the local Krack-A-Joke shop, a well-known place for local magicians. This was the greatest Christmas gift ever. This little figure was very nice, but in time, I grew bored with it as it wasn't very big, not a real professional-sized dummy. So I began to modify it, adding hair and repainting and so on. I decided to have a go at trying to build my own character, a much more challenging job than I had realized. I found a book at the joke shop by Paul Winchell on ventriloquism and how to carve your own puppet—*Ventriloquism for Fun and Profit*. It was a beginning, but sadly, the instructions on carving and other details were incomplete, just not detailed enough, and I was running into problems with my project. The trouble also was my tools, too small for such a large carving piece. I wasn't getting anywhere fast, and I was becoming frustrated with my progress.

My first visit to the ventriloquist's museum, Vent Haven, located in Fort Mitchell, Kentucky, in 1984. This photo is of me with the replica dolls of Bergen's famous duo, Charlie and Mortimer.

Around 1953, my school art classes were working with a modelling compound that we made up from white flour, water, and asbestos powder. We weren't aware at the time that asbestos was dangerous, and it was a common item for clay modelling in elementary school classes in the '50s. I crafted a puppet head, complete with moving mouth and hands, all in this asbestos clay. It was an ugly little guy, but I was proud of it and was having a great time with my first Clarence. One day I was giving a little performance at my home for a birthday party, after which I placed Clarence on a stool for all to admire. Before I realized what was happening, he slowly tipped forward and fell to the floor with a sickening crunch, smashed into bits. *Oh no!*

Aside from that disaster, it was my first attempt at building a puppet, and I could see the possibilities. I was a determined kid. But I really needed help to continue working on my wooden-headed Clarence that had stalled out weeks earlier.

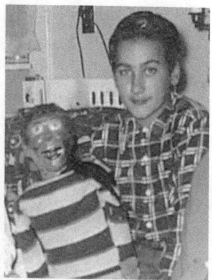

Pictured here on the left is my Jerry Mahoney, and on the right is my first attempt at building a character using asbestos, not a good thing given what we know today about the hazards of asbestos.

Clarence number two. After some hard work and help from my friend
Mr. Steinman, this was the result. Clarence featured walking legs, a
design of Steinman's that I adapted to my figure.

Here is Clarence number three, and I can't help but see a resemblance between me and the puppet. This puppet is still in use and had been my main character for over ten years, up until my present character Noseworthy, which came into the show in 1965 and has been my main working puppet up to this day.

Paul Winchell's earlier book *Ventriloquism for Fun and Profit*, which got me started back in 1953. I learned the basics of ventriloquism and some idea of carving a wooden figure. It got me started. However, the figure-building directions were not very detailed, and it wasn't until I met my teacher, Mr. Steinman, that I actually had some instruction on figure carving and building. From there on, I continued to develop my carving skills and eventually become a competent figure builder.

This was in 1952, and I continued to work away at my puppet project. Progress was very slow, and at times, I felt I was never going to get this puppet finished. I needed help. That help came to me quite unexpectedly during a visit to a toy shop in Vancouver in December. Here, I met Mr. Steinman, who was performing with his puppet band in the shop window. After meeting him and his "band," he kindly offered to show me his workshop and projects, puppets he was working on. I visited his home a number of times over the coming year and learned firsthand the techniques and methods of figure building.

As a result of these visits and many hours of my struggling with my wood-carving project, I eventually had completed my first carved puppet head, Clarence, some months later. This was the beginning of a friendship that lasted until Mr. Steinman passed away a few years later. To my knowledge, I am the only one he ever showed how to create ventriloquist dolls. The ironic thing is I was never able to own one of his creations. To this day, I do not know what became of his remaining collection of figures. I found out that some were donated to a local history museum of Vancouver, but most were back in Ontario with some family members.

Clarence, first carved figure, 1955.

Mr. Steinman with his star character, building
a birdhouse. My teacher and mentor.

The movie *Magic* came out in 1978, a story about a ventriloquist
who was controlled by his murderous dummy, Fats, with Anthony
Hopkins and his love interest, Anne Margaret. This was typical of

the type of movies that featured a ventriloquist who was psychotic, creating a creepy aspect to ventriloquism, which has made some people, to this day, literally afraid of ventriloquist puppets. If that wasn't bad enough, the next puppet/doll movie that really freaked people out was *Chucky*, again a murderous doll in what was a nightmare horror movie, a popular series yet—bad PR for us poor ventriloquists.

It is interesting to note that traditionally, ventriloquists and their sidekicks were essentially a comedy team, the ventriloquist being the straight man and the puppet the wisecracking partner who brought gales of laughter from their audiences. It has traditionally been a wonderful illusion where the character seems to come alive and is a quick-witted scoundrel, always getting one over the straight man, the ventriloquist. To their credit, Edgar Bergen and Paul Winchell did much to dispel the dark side of the art and made it a family entertainment and, in Bergen's case, on radio yet! In the tradition of the craft, from those early years, I have borrowed from Bergen and Winchell their wonderful, whimsical performances that have stood the test of time. As dated as some of the material is, it still is very enjoyable to listen to the old shows, be it on radio or early television. I still find inspiration from those performances.

Paul Winchell with his sidekick Jerry Mahoney, 1960s.

Bergen's characters before restoration for
installation at the Smithsonian.

This photo was taken a few months after Bergen's passing. The
puppets were in the care of a friend of mine who was commissioned
to restore the dolls for their display at the Smithsonian Museum.

What a huge event for me to actually have the characters
in my hands, quite historic and at the same time a sad
tribute to a great artist and inspiration to me.

Bergen was in Vancouver as a guest star in a local series called *The Littlest Hobo*, a feel-good series about a dog and his adventures in a small town where the dog would help rescue people and help the local police round up criminals. Bergen was cast as a visiting sideshow performer in the town, and my dad was cast as a bartender in the film. This was how I got to meet Mr. Bergen through my dad's acquaintance with him.

During his stay in Vancouver for the film shoot, I was able to meet with Mr. Bergen. He invited me to dinner at his hotel in town. He knew from my dad that I had built a puppet, so he asked me if I had it with me, which I did, under the table in the suitcase. Right there in the restaurant, I did an impromptu bit. He kindly corrected my technique. I had no idea really what I was doing, so starstruck at the moment. He later responded with this note he sent to me. What a huge compliment!

Bergen sent me this autographed photo after we met in Vancouver where he was working on a film project with my dad . The series: The Littlest Hobo.

Bergen sent me this autographed photo after we met in Vancouver, where he was working on a film project with my dad, the series *The Littlest Hobo*.

Chapter Two

Ventriloquism Introduction

Here is a quick summary of the course. I have laid out **the details of developing a unique character of your own design.**

- The vocal magic of making it sound and look like your puppet is **a personality and speaking in its own voice**

- The tricks and vocal techniques of ventriloquism

- The different voices, near and distant

- Details of woodcarving and figure construction

- Designing and building your own character

- Methods of detailing and creating an original character in the traditional lost art of figure building

- Animation and the manipulation of a puppet character

- Presentation and stagecraft plus ideas and information on writing and creating a show

Inspiration for this book began when, after many years of working and developing the act, I realized that I needed to create a history and story of how I began my career as a professional ventriloquist. It was time to take a closer look at this business of talking to myself and playing with dolls and how my act and love of ventriloquism evolved and became my passion for the past fifty years.

What started me thinking about a book on the subject of ventriloquism?

While working on a cruise ship, I had a conversation with a passenger who was fascinated with the whole idea of ventriloquism and wanted to know if I had a book on the subject. In addition, my wife and sister have been after me for many years to get busy and create this book. So I think it was about time I put pen to paper (finger to keyboard) and got started. This book is a result of that inspiration. I felt it was time I put back into the art what I have learned and benefited from over the years, sharing with you some of the stories and travels that have made for a very interesting career and certainly lots of fun, not to mention some of the amazing and talented people I have had the pleasure of meeting and working with over the years, also a very nice way to make a living through my many years of performing in all kinds of venues, in a variety of situations, some good and some of them downright awful. It is to be hoped that what I have learned will help and inspire you get the most out of this fascinating craft.

The Early Days

Beginning with the story of how I got into this life of a ventriloquist performer, it was a lifelong dream, I guess, from when I first heard the radio shows of Edgar Bergen and Charlie McCarthy in the 1950s to Paul Winchell on television in the mid-fifties to the present day, and that was a very long time ago.

To give you some background on my journey, I thought I should write about the early days, my childhood fantasies and boyhood adventure of creating puppets. It became such a driving force in my early years, I never stopped chasing after the dream of becoming a ventriloquist with my own puppet creations.

The main objective of this book is to teach you about ventriloquism and figure building. If you are anything like me when I was younger, you will consume everything you can find about the subject, and back in those early years, there wasn't that much to be found, at least not for a young boy of thirteen and with very limited resources and, need I mention, Google, Facebook, and YouTube were none existent. Now everything is in a computer in your pocket. Information on anything you want to know is all there. I had a very old copy of a book on ventriloquism written by Paul Winchell and the encyclopedia where I could find a bit more information. Other than that, I was watching television for ventriloquists and saw a number who inspired me, kept my interest alive. Now I feel it is my turn to contribute something back to a career and art that has given me so much.

When I first took an interest in ventriloquism, the most commonly used character was the young smart-aleck kid, the cheeky boy doll. This type was typical and used by the two most famous vents working at that time, Edgar Bergen with Charlie McCarthy and Paul Winchell with his sidekick, Jerry Mahoney.

Bergen and Winchell established these types with the public through their early performances on radio in the '30s until the beginning of television when Winchell rose to popularity in the '50s. This is the classic style, with the character always getting the laugh at the expense of the vent.

When you consider that Bergen's performances were mostly on radio, you have to believe that Charlie was a real personality. He seemed to have a life of his own, an amazing feat when you consider the medium that Bergen was working in. A ventriloquist on radio? Today that would seem almost absurd. What Bergen accomplished was quite amazing and is a tribute to his talent and the writing. The shows were very entertaining and listened to by millions of people for over twelve years, one of the most popular radio shows at the time.

I still find these old shows fun to listen to and am always inspired by the technique and characters created by Bergen and Winchell. The character separation from the ventriloquist was so complete that if you did not know this was a ventriloquist and his puppet, you would believe that Charlie and Jerry were real people. If you can get an opportunity to listen to some of these older broadcasts, good idea. Facebook—go there and type in "ventriloquism." You will find all the greats of the past and present, and yours truly is in there too.

Other vents at the time would often appear on the big variety shows of the day, mainly the *Ed Sullivan Show*. That show was a Sunday-evening ritual at my home. There, I witnessed many vents over the years, and all of them inspired me. During this time, I was diligently working my way through a book on ventriloquism that I found at the school library. This was in 1953, and I was a kid with a big ambition to become a ventriloquist no matter what. I was learning the technique, doing a self-taught course from the book. I didn't have any instructor to guide me or even a puppet to work with. I decided that I had to try and build a dummy. Paul Winchell's book *Ventriloquism for Fun and Profit* had a section on building a puppet. That was a guide, and I was trying to carve a head from this large block of wood. With inadequate tools and little know-how, I struggled for months and had very little to show for efforts.

My father bought me a Jerry Mahoney doll, a figure that was about three quarters of the full size of the original and had a moving mouth and head. It was wonderful! However, it was not long before I was reworking the figure to my specifications—new paint, hair, clothes, etc. I wanted my own original version.

This was in 1955, and I was fourteen years old and had some ability to carve and sculpt, along with my meagre talents and tools. I was working from Paul Winchell's book on how to be a vent and build dummies. I didn't make much progress but had fun trying. I did succeed in building a moulded head from a compound made up of flour, water, and asbestos. This product is now banned from use, but back then, it was used in schools as a modelling compound. Can you imagine that? That first puppet was inspired by my imagination and the photos I had of Bergen's Charlie and other figures I had seen in films at the time.

The result was an ugly puppet, but it worked. I called him Clarence, and he had one performance. Then he fell off the chair and smashed into a hundred pieces. He was a "one-trick pony" for sure. You can imagine my shock as I saw my creation destroyed before my eyes. I have only one photo of this early Clarence, the first of three that I eventually carved in wood. Each new figure was an improvement over its predecessor. My parents felt sorry for me and replaced Clarence with a brand new Jerry Mahoney figure. He was three quarters of the full size, with a snazzy sports coat, and was a half-size replica of Paul Winchell's partner. That was the best Christmas present I had ever had in my thirteen years. It was not long before I began to modify the character—new hair, repainted eyes and face. I could not leave well enough alone. I had a talent for building things. I loved to sculpt, draw, and paint. The artist in me was always looking for a chance to improve or modify what I had.

Winchell had published a book around that time, *Ventriloquism for Fun and Profit*, with a section on how to build/carve a vent doll. I was soon busy in the basement workshop working away at my newest puppet creation, Clarence number two. I had a large block of wood and a set of very small carving tools. My progress was painfully slow. I was determined and kept whittling away for days without much to show for my efforts.

During that December, I, by chance, met an old gentleman in a toy shop in Vancouver who was demonstrating his amazing dummy band. All his characters were animated mechanically and played musical instruments in time to a recorded song playing on a phonograph. I was amazed at what I saw. Mr. Steinman, it turns out, was a master figure carver and was well known internationally as one of the best builders in the business at that time. He was quite old then and only built a few figures for a few of his select customers. Bergen would visit his workshop from time to time for repairs to his characters whenever he was in the area. As I got to know him, we became student and teacher. He invited me to his home and workshop to observe him working on various projects. I was unofficially his student of figure making. Little did he know that one day I was to become the only person who was to carry on his craft and techniques that he had developed.

Our friendship lasted until he passed away several years later. I never owned any of his work. As a young boy with few resources in my family, I couldn't afford to buy any of his puppets. To this day, I don't know what happened to the puppets he had in his collection. His nephew somewhere inherited them back east, and I never was able to find out who or where that person was located. Somewhere his masterpieces are packed away in someone's attic, I might assume. Maybe one day they will turn up. Peter Rolston and Dick Gardener, two local vents, were owners of Steinman's figures in those early days. Both are gone now, and as far as I know, they were the only ventriloquists in the Pacific Northwest who had examples of his work. I know that Pop had produced a number of figures over the years, but where they reside now is a mystery to me. Even the Ventriloquist's Museum and fraternity know very little about him to this day. He was unique and, in my humble opinion, one of the best.

In those early days, there was very little information available to me on ventriloquism. Computers hadn't been invented yet, and the few vents who were around in my town were just not available to me. I didn't know who they were, so for a youngster, it was all a world of mystery. I consumed everything I could find that had to do with ventriloquism—any photos, films, and books and, of course, what I saw on television. The best variety show in its time was the *Ed Sullivan Show*. There was always a ventriloquist turning up, and I was a big fan of the show.I was obsessed with the puppets. I wanted to carve and build as many as I could. The actual performing came later as I began to be asked to do shows in my community at the time. We lived in a small town in the province of British Columbia, Penticton. I had entered my carved character a few years later, Clarence, in a local talent/hobby show and won first prize—but not without some comment that "I really didn't build this myself," that I was basically "cheating" *What?* I was fifteen years old, I was pretty upset but soon got over that and went on to performing and building other puppets. This was in 1955, and for the record, it was there that I performed my first paying gig in Penticton for five dollars. Wow! I actually got paid for something I loved to do! I guess that belief is still with me. However, my fees have gone up a bit since then.

Chapter Three

Origins of Ventriloquism: A Brief History

How far back are the origins of ventriloquism, and who were the earliest practitioners of the art?

Although ventriloquy (for *ventriloquism*; the words are interchangeable) is today a form of humorous entertainment, the origin of the term lies in a practice that was deadly serious and more than just a little creepy. The word "ventriloquism" comes from the Latin *ventriloquus*, meaning speaking from the belly (*venter* plus *loqui*, "speak"). So "speaking from the belly" is a plausible metaphor for ventriloquism.

But *ventriloquus* was no metaphor. It was believed by the ancient Greeks (who called the phenomenon *eggastrimuthos*) and Romans that noises emanating from a person's belly could be the voices of the spirits of the dead or, worse, a sign of demonic possession. A ventriloquist (later called a "gastromancer") was a seer or psychic who interpreted the sounds coming from the person's abdomen and, depending on the supposed source, passed along predictions of the future, messages from the future. Like early magic, the secrets of ventriloquism were closely guarded, especially in the times when vent was practiced as a black art, used by mystics, priests, and conjurers. The Egyptians learned ventriloquism, it is presumed by the priests, to create the effect that the spirits of the dead and their gods were speaking to the populace. A few oracles were highly skilled ventriloquists; they would use the voices to invoke prophecies, to give predictions of outcomes of events, wars, etc. The early Greeks did the same, practiced the art called gastronomy, a form of ventriloquism imitating the sounds of animals and other deities of the times.

Ventriloquism and Gastromancy: Europe and America

Eventually, however, the public ardor for spiritualism flowered into the age of stage magic. The term *ventriloquism* came to be the trick of "throwing one's voice" as an entertainment for an audience. By the late nineteenth century, "ventriloquy" was a standard act in the repertoire of vaudeville, and the wooden ventriloquist's dummy became an icon of popular culture.

Interestingly, however, ventriloquy has never been able to completely shed its overtones of creepiness as the number of horror movies involving a murderous dummy that takes over the poor deranged ventriloquist and goes on a murderous rampage. The ventriloquist, unable to control the horrific events, is caught up in the illusion of the puppet being a living character. Even to this day, I know of some ventriloquists who have a hard time drawing a line between the reality and fantasy and actually have a strange relationship with their puppet character. actually having arguments with the puppet and referring to them as a person, like "he" or "she," and using their names as you might when talking about a living person.

Pop Steinman with his dummy band performing in his home for the neighbourhood children with his wife by his side. This was the little band I first saw back in 1953 when I met Mr. Steinman. It was the beginning of a friendship that led me to learning ventriloquism and building puppets.

Barney, a character I created back in 1973, influenced by Mr. Steinman, my mentor and teacher. The figure below is a typical example of his style of figure design that has influenced my work, as you can see by the similarities of the two characters.

It was claimed, as written in the Bible, that a king was told by a "witch" the outcome of a battle. The witch created the voice of the prophet Samuel, who was to have spoken from the dead, answering the king's questions. We assume the witch was no doubt an accomplished ventriloquist.

The Pacific Islanders were followers of their priests and were superstitious believers of their religions and rites. They would listen to their idols speaking. The Eskimo peoples were also known to be practitioners of ventriloquism. Not until the 1800s did ventriloquism start to become an entertainment. Some of the earliest known puppets were more like clockwork automatons. These creations were very complex mechanical puppets that operated much in the way a watch does. Built as novel curiosities, these marvels of mechanical innovation were sometimes used by ventriloquists as their puppets. Some early ventriloquists were very skilled at imitating animal and other curious sounds, sometimes known as polyphonists.

Vent figures became popular in the 1800s during the Edwardian and Victorian Eras. Figures were often dressed as sailors and soldiers. It was a vent by the name of Fred Russell who was credited with the first knee figure, Coster Joe, in about 1840. He is claimed to be the father of modern ventriloquism. Way to go, Fred!

At the turn of the century, the early 1900s, a number of prominent vents made their mark, such as Arthur Prince in 1900. John Cooper, the first known black ventriloquist, was very innovative, using several figures in a barbershop setting, each one operated with hand-and-foot controls. The Great Lester (1904) was Edgar Bergen's mentor and teacher, in his time a well-known performer and innovator of the ventriloquist's craft. Bergen brought new popularity to the art as he worked the vaudeville circuit and fairs throughout the United States, earning his way to a medical diploma at the Northwestern University. His puppet, Charlie McCarthy, was in inspiration of a newspaper carrier boy Bergen had met at one time. He had the character built by a part-time figure maker and carver, Charlie Mac, in Chicago in about 1930.

The Vent Haven Museum on my visit in 1996.

This photo shows me with Noseworthy sitting in with some very historic ventriloquist puppets, only a small part of the museum collection. This group of characters reminds of some of the audiences I have encountered over the years, wide-eyed and totally focused, more like a bizarre, hypnotized group of people.

Bergen has been an inspiration to many aspiring ventriloquists, including myself. His radio and film work over the years reached around the world. Charlie and Mortimer were so much a part of American popular culture and history, they have been preserved for posterity at the Smithsonian in Washington. Bergen passed away in Las Vegas one evening after a show, ironically his comeback tour, in 1978. Mr. Bergen was not only a brilliant vent but also an inspiration to many young vents over the years, including myself. I had the good fortune of meeting him in Vancouver in 1969. He was impressed with my figure-building talents, encouraged me to keep at it, and would recommend me to inquiring vents as a figure builder. Mr. Bergen was always very approachable and personally answered his fan mail. He was always the gentleman and professional.

This illustration of an early practitioner of ventriloquism making it sound like a pig was talking.

In 1945, Paul Winchell, with his characters Jerry Mahoney and Knucklehead Smiff, followed Bergen in the early era of television. Mr. Winchell died in 2006 and was, up till then, a very active member of the ventriloquist's fraternity and was always working on innovations. His book *Ventriloquism for Fun and Profit* came out in 1950 and was a big inspiration to me. He also produced a very good video course on ventriloquism, featuring clips of his television shows of the '50s. Unfortunately, all the videotapes of his shows were destroyed by the network. As a result, very little film is available of Paul's work. His characters were built by renowned figure maker Frank Marshall out of Chicago. He was responsible for the creation of many vent figures and supplied the majority of amateur and working vents of the time—Jimmy Nelson and Paul Winchell, to name just a couple. Their legacy lives on. Some of these famous puppet characters are now at the Vent Haven Museum in Fort Mitchell, Kentucky.

The Ventriloquist Convention 2016 in Cincinnati a few years ago, me with the amazing Bob Rhumba, a very talented and creative guy. That was the best convention, thanks to Mark Wade and his group of hardworking members. They keep producing the convention year after year, and it just gets bigger and better. This is a fun photo of me and Bob Rhumba, his "mini-mees," and my Noseworthy.

Ventriloquism: What Is It? How Is It Done? Can Anyone Do It?

Fact and Fiction

There is no such thing as throwing your voice. Your vocal sounds cannot be made to come from a distant source. There are no gimmicks or special whistles that create the illusion. You can, however, create the illusion of sounds, voices that are coming from another source. Ventriloquism is a form of sound mimicry, the art of misdirection. I call it the "vocal magic" of ventriloquism.

That is ventriloquism, making people believe the voices they hear are coming from another source.

The good news is anyone with a normal speaking voice can learn ventriloquism. It is the same as learning to sing, playing a musical instrument, or mastering a new performance skill. You need to learn the basic technique. With practice, you will master the methods. The longer you work at it, the better you will become. It will require some dedication and a bit of work, but in a few months, you should have it.

In the early days, people used to think that the voice came from their stomach or that you have a double throat or some other form of physical anomaly. The methods of creating the voices and illusion was a closely guarded secret among the practitioners of the art. It was considered a magical gift, even witchcraft in the early days.

The word *ventriloquism* is derived from the Latin words *ventre*, which means "stomach," and *loqui*, which means "to speak"—translated "to speak from the stomach." The sound comes from your vocal cords. The abdominal muscles are used for the correct breathing. Nasal passages also play a part in creating the illusion of distance and give a distinct resonance to the ventriloquial voice. However, the sound only comes from your vocal cords and not from your stomach. Like a magician, the ventriloquist uses misdirection. I call it the "sleight of voice" or, as I said, "vocal magic."

The fact is, hearing is not one of our most reliable senses. You need to see where you believe the voice or sound is coming from. In the case of the ventriloquist's doll, the character animation and mouth movement completes the illusion; hence, we believe or assume the doll is speaking.

The use of a microphone enhances the illusion. Some vents even have a "dummy" microphone placed in front of the doll to help complete the effect. I will discuss further in later chapters about performance and production for the stage. It is now time to begin the fun project of learning ventriloquism, beginning with the basic vocal techniques used in creating this fascinating illusionary art.

So let us get started.

Chapter Four

Lesson Number One

Vocalization

The Voices

There are three basic ventriloquist's voices:

- Near

- Near distant (radio, talking watch, voice in a box, etc.)

- Distant

I will begin with the near voice, the most commonly used technique. Later, we can go into the other effects in more detail. The puppet voice, the character's voice combined with the animation, completes the illusion of the puppet speaking. This is the typical near-voice technique and the most commonly practiced and the easiest to learn.

The more advanced vocal techniques, near distant and distant, will be explored more completely as we progress. The near distant voice or muffled effect is what vents use when the character is in a case, for example, also for effects onstage where the puppet may be a little distance away from the operator, but the quality of the sound is altered to give an effect of distance. The faraway voices, as in the distant voice method, is used when we want an offstage voice or sound coming from below, upstairs, outside, from a faraway source, etc. In addition, this small voice is the same used for, say, a telephone or radio effect. These more advanced methods require more practice and some play-acting on the part of the vent to enhance the illusion they are trying to create.

Learning ventriloquism is a technique most anyone can learn. It will take dedication and practice to get it right. I suppose you might say it is more difficult than learning to ride a bike or roller blades and a lot less painful than trying to stop rollerblading down a hill for the first time. It is a skill most anyone can learn, really!

Like any other art form, it takes practice and dedication to perfect your craft. The basics of ventriloquism, however, can be acquired within a reasonable amount of time. To begin, it means learning the alphabet without moving your lips, developing a character voice that is different from your own, creating the illusion of the voice coming from another source. Oh, you thought vents actually threw their voice? That is the common belief, but in fact, you are only creating the appearance of a voice coming from a distant or other source. This effect is based on some fundamental facts about our ability to hear sounds and determine the source of those sounds. Our hearing is not that accurate. We need visual clues as to the source of the sound.

Now to clarify among the different vent voices we will learn about. To begin with, the question is, how far can you throw your voice? The answer is, as far as you can hear me. It is, in fact, vocal mimicry, creating the sound (illusion) of a distant voice. As mentioned earlier, the ventriloquist's voices are divided into three categories: near; near distant, muffled as in a suitcase, for example; and distant, e.g., telephone, radio, far away, or echo.

The *near* voice is the one you will learn first, the voice most easily perfected, used when operating a puppet close to you. The *near-distant* voice is the modified method, giving the effect of a voice coming out of a suitcase or box or behind a wall, somewhat removed from the vent, hence the old trick of the dummy in the suitcase yelling, "Hey, let me outta here!"

The *distant* voice is the more difficult technique and is learned after you have perfected the other two, near and near distant, methods. People hearing a voice in the distance, across the street, or far away to the point that you can barely make out what is being said exemplify this method. Now we will get into how to create these effects.

Just before we get started, I will outline the main elements of the method, technique, and practice.

The Ventriloquists' "Drone"

Lip Control

The Alphabet

The ventriloquist's alphabet entails learning the proper methods of pronunciation, especially for the more difficult letters, such as B, F, M, P, U, V, W, and Y. These are the ones we will work on and master.

We then move on to the character voice, how to find your "inner voice," as it were. The near voice and near-distant and distant voice methods will be explored and techniques learned and practiced as we progress.

The other fun stuff will be developing your puppet or, if you like, your "alter ego." Assuming you want to work with a puppet, you need to learn manipulation and the animation to bring your character to life and then coordinating all these elements to create the reality and personality of your puppet partner, not to mention your own development with an integral role of an opposing character in the duo, which usually means you are the straight man, and the character (puppet), the comic, gets all the good lines and laughs, hopefully.

The Ventriloquists' Drone and Lip Control

This is a sound that you make like a humming, only it comes from the back of the throat. It sounds like an "ehhh" sound. Think of a bee buzzing. This is the basis of the voice you will be using for the puppet voice. Curl your tongue up to partially block the sound. The more you block/restrict the sound, the smaller the voice sounds, hence a more distant quality to the sound. The effect you have on your vocal/distant is affected by the resonating of the sound in your nasal passages and head. This effect makes it difficult for a listener to determine the source of the sound. Having said that, your mouth needs to be opened a bit for this. Practice the drone in a vocal sound that comes through your mouth and nose. It has a somewhat nasal quality to it. The voices you produce this way will be closer to the distant sound but when opened up more becomes the near voice, which you will be using most of the time and is the more easily learned of the three voices. The drone is the very basic sound that you will be using and later modifying to produce the other voices.

At this point, I would recommend using a voice-recording device to record your sounds and vocalizations. This will help you in your vocal clarity of the alphabet sounds. A mirror would also be helpful; this way, you can watch your lip movement and keep an eye on your improvement and development.

Regarding lip control, I will have covered this to an extent later on the course. However, it is very important that you pay very close attention to this, for without excellent lip control, a lot of the illusion is lost, not to mention your credibility as a competent ventriloquist.

"Aren't ventriloquists supposed to keep their mouths closed when the puppet is speaking?" Yes, I have witnessed far too many ventriloquists who think that lip control is not of primary importance or just an option so as long as the puppet is funny and the material is good. Sorry, but that doesn't cut it. Now if you are a puppeteer, that is a different matter. They are usually hidden behind a set screen and not interacting with the puppet characters. They can move their lips, and no one would see it—no illusion to worry about. However, a vent has to be solid and technically skilled with no lip movement, as perfect as can be, hence a better illusion. You get the point? No lip movement, none. Now this is where you need to practice the methods I have laid down here in this course.

To begin with—and take note—fact is, you don't completely close your mouth. Your teeth are not clenched together as no sound would escape and you couldn't be heard clearly—just a mad clenched teeth sound, you know, like when your mother used to get really mad at you and yell at you through clenched teeth, "Donny, you stop that clowning right now!" So let it be known—you have to have some opening, teeth and lips, just a little bit. Many vents use a smile to set their mouths, sometimes with the upper teeth resting on the lower lip. This way, sounds come through between the lips, also through your nasal cavities, your nose. So you think the bigger the nose, the better the effect? No, not really. I have a rather large nose, and I don't believe it has helped me. Then again, maybe it has a bigger resonating chamber.

Mark Wade and yours truly at the Ventriloquist Convention 2016 in Cincinnati. He has been the organizer for the convention for over twenty-three years whom I know of. This was the best convention I have attended so far. They get better each successive year. Congratulations, Mark.

The problem, however, with a fixed smile on your face every time the puppet is speaking is you have this goofy grin on your face, even if you are supposed to be angry with the character. So in addition to the smile technique, also practice a deadpan expression and still have the character voice coming through. You can also change your expression as the character is speaking, appearing to be reacting to what the puppet is saying. Create a separation of characters. You're the straight man; he's the wise guy, noisy kid, oddball, cranky old dude, nice church lady, whatever. Keep things interesting. This appears a lot more natural than grinning all the time.

Remember you are the opposite of the puppet. Try to define your character in the role you play. Are you strict, easygoing, classy with an air about you, like you are some superior being, or are you two buddies and have a chummy relationship? Think about who you are in the duo. Play your role. You don't have to overact. Just find a character that is a side of you and work it in contrast to your partner. Be that someone, your stage persona, whom you are comfortable with. It took me a lot of years to stop hiding behind my puppet and become a personality of my own. I was shy and not comfortable on stage without my "prop." In time, I was able to gain confidence in my ability and talent.

Lesson Number Two

The Ventriloquists' Alphabet

Pronunciation of the letters of the alphabet is the key for learning good technique. After you have practiced the "drone," we can now move on to the letters that form the words we refer to as the ventriloquists' vocal scale. The most easily pronounced words to produce without lip movement are the consonants C, G, H, J, K, L, Q, S, T, X, and Z. The vowels—A, E, I, O, and U—come to mind as an easy practice for the less difficult sounds. The labials, which require practiced lip control technique, will be B, F, M, P, R, V, W, and Y. The normal way of pronouncing the easy letters can be done fairly easily without lip movement. Practicing these in front of the mirror will prove to be easy to master.

At this point, I should again mention something about your mouth. Think about the expression on your face while speaking in the puppet's voice. It is very common for many vents to set their mouth in a wide smile, with teeth flashing. This helps keep the lips taut and in control, but it does look a bit strange. People are not always grinning like that when listening to someone else speaking. You would tend to look a bit strange, unnatural.

You need to register some emotion and other expressions while your character is speaking. You need to show some expressions other than a pasted-on smile. Your mouth needs to have a minimum gap, an opening to let the sound out. You cannot speak with your mouth completely closed. It may look as though a vent is speaking with his mouth closed, but it isn't. I find that a relaxed neutral expression is good for the most part, keeping a gap in the middle of the mouth or at the sides. Rest you lower lip gently on your upper teeth to help keep the mouth from moving or quivering while speaking. This position also allows for openings at the corners of your mouth. The sound comes through your mouth and nasal passages. A combination of both exits gives the puppet voice a "detached sound," a quality you are looking for.

What you will be learning is how to speak without lips, using your tongue and teeth to form letters and words. This is a very handy skill. How often have we wished we could talk without people seeing our mouth move? With ventriloquism, you will learn this plus the added effect of the voice appearing to come from another place, in or under an object, or, of course, from your puppet partner.

Getting back to the alphabet, what I want you to do is sit in front of the mirror and go through the easy letters—A, E, C, G, H, I, J, K, L, O, Q, R, S, T, U, X, Z—first with lips moving as in normal pronunciation. Listen to yourself on your recorder. Do the sounds seem correct to you? Now go through them again without moving your lips. Go over them and watch for lip movement. While speaking the sounds, think about how you use your tongue to form the letters. In most instances, with the letters shown above, there is little movement required of the lips.

The letter A — Hold your lips still, and say the letter A. Say this by dropping your jaw open. Notice you can still say the letter without moving your lips if you just drop your tongue down to the bottom of your mouth, which gives the same effect as opening your mouth.

At this point, do not worry too much about the character voice. It is okay to use one if you think you have already nailed a voice that comes easily to you. Just be sure it is different from yours. It should be a higher or lower pitch than your own. If you are able to change the accent or develop a speech with a different rhythm from yours, that is very good. Anything that sets the character voice apart from your own adds to the illusion.

Keep in mind too what kind of character you want to have sitting on your knee. Is it a boy or girl? Old? Young? An animal? Whatever it may be, use this as the basis for your vent voice. I will go into more about character development later on. For now, find a working voice that you can practice and develop.

I got off the track there a bit, so now let us return to the alphabet and work on those easier letters a while. After that, we will tackle the more difficult B, F, M, N, P, V, W, and Y.

Did you manage okay with the A? That is a simple sound to create without lip movement. Remember to keep the lower teeth lightly touching the upper lip, but do not clench your teeth together. Never at any time do you lock your jaw so that the teeth are closed. Your mouth needs to be slightly open at either the corners or the centre for the sound to escape. A slight smile or a neutral expression is fine; even if you are frowning, you can still keep the mouth in the correct position, allowing the sound to escape. Remember to use the mirror and your sound recorder to monitor yourself.

The letter E — This will come easy as it is pronounced normally. No lip problem here; keep the letter sound long—"Eeeee."

The letter C — The letter is again pronounced by placing the tip of the tongue up and then dropped down. No lips required here—"Ceeee."

The letter D — Pronounce this by pressing the tongue up against the roof of your mouth and then dropping the tip down sharply. This works well without lips and sounds the same as if you were speaking normally.

The letter G — You will find this pronounced by bringing the tongue down and drawing out the "eee"—"Geee." At the beginning, you will want to drop your jaw to open the mouth to say the G. You can make a G sound without that movement.

The letter H — This letter begins with A and ends with "ch," a long sound on the A and short sound on the "ch." The tongue goes up and then down. As in normal speech, you will find that the tip of the tongue is used a lot while making these sounds.

The letter I — This is spoken as in normal speech. The tongue drops down and will sound like *eye*.

The letter J — The sound is like *jay*. The tongue stays low in the mouth and ends with a long "aaay" sound.

The letter K — This sound has a sound at the beginning that is made by bringing the tongue down sharply from the sides with "kuh" and adding the "aay." The sound is made as normal—"kaaay." Just keep your jaw from dropping. Run the sounds together. "Kaaay."

The letter L — This sound is produced by starting with the "eh" sound and then bringing tip of the tongue up and sharply down. Put together, it is pronounced "ehll." The letter N — This starts with the sound "eh" and then the N sound. Again, the tongue is low, and at the N sound, bring the tip up sharply. Together, it sounds like "ehhn."

The letter O — Saying the letter O is done the same as you would normally say it, but will not form your lips into an O shape. Just say, "Ohhh." The volume of the mouth is increased when you drop your tongue down, giving a bigger, more open sound. With practice, it will sound exactly like the letter.

The letter Q — It is said as "keuw." You will find this one works very easily without lip movement. Practice it a few times, and it will come out sounding right, no lips needed. Emphasize on the K with a long "euw."

The letter R — It is pronounced as "ahhrr." The tongue starts low— "ahh"—and then the tip comes up sharply on the R, the same as normal speech but without the lips, As the pirates once said, "Arrr, matey!"

The letter S — Starts with the "ehh" and then ends with "sss," a hissing sound, Together, it is "ehss." The tongue is up at the sides. The tip comes up to form the hissing sound. Practice and pay attention to what the tongue is doing when normal speech is used. The hissing sound is the sound of air blowing through the space between the tip of the tongue and teeth. You can produce this effect without lip movement. Keep the lower lip in light contact with the upper teeth; let the sound escape at the corners or the middle of your mouth.

The letter T — You make the "tuh-ee" sound by putting the tongue behind the front teeth and dropping down sharply to get the "tuh" sound when produced normally. The jaw is dropped slightly as the tongue drops. You can still achieve this by using the tip of the tongue only. Say the "tuh" sound, add the "eee," and smooth it out. Running the sounds together will give you the T sound. The emphasis is on the "tuh."

You will notice the letter sounds are produced right up behind the front teeth. Often beginners will try to suppress the sound and move it farther back into the mouth. Keep the sounds up front right behind the front teeth and at the tip of your tongue. All the action is right behind your teeth. As I mentioned earlier, you are learning to speak without the lips. Your tongue and teeth do all the work of forming the letters.

The letter U — When forming the letter U, we have a tendency to pucker our lips to give the "ooo" sound. This sound can also be made without the lips. Say, "Yooo." Hold the lips flat and still. The sound will come out as the letter U.

The letter X — It is said as "ekss," with emphasis on the "ek" sound and then followed by a long "sss" sound. The tongue tip moves down for the "ek" and then up for the "sss" sound. Now smooth it out to sound like the letter X.

The letter Z — It sounds like either of two ways: "zeee" or "zed," depending on where you come from, "zeee" being the easier of the two to pronounce without lips. Say the letter normally, with lips moving and then with lips held still. It isn't that much different. Either way, just keep the lips frozen.

Now we move on to the more difficult letters: B, F, M, P, V, W, and Y. These letters will require more practice and tricks to pronounce. There are two methods used in forming these letters. One method is to use letter substitutions—for example, using D to sound like a B. I find this method confusing and harder to convince the listener that you are actually saying the letter B. It is best to learn how to pronounce the letter with your tongue and teeth to form the proper sound without the lips or substitution sounds.

The letter B — In normal speech, the lips start the letter sound with an explosive parting to get the "buh" sound and then adds the "eee" sounds, with emphasis on the "eee." Say the letter moving your lips, record it, and listen to the sound you have made. Use this as a guide when pronouncing the letter without lips.

It helps to remember that you will be using your tongue and upper teeth to replace the action of your lips of opening and closing your mouth. If you flatten your tongue and place it at the edge of your front teeth, you are now creating the substitute lips. You can also try placing the tip of your tongue, curled slightly, at the back of the upper gum line. When you drop the tongue down as you say B, you should get a sound close to the proper sound of B. When saying the "buh" part, push some air behind the sound. It will come out more explosive. It will at first sound more like a D, but practice will smooth it out. Use the recorder to listen to your progress. It is tricky to get the exact sounds, but it is the most effective method of sound creation of the "expletive" letters.

You will find that when you are speaking with the lips still, the difficult letter sounds are more easily understood when used in a sentence. For example, "This is a bigger house" will sound more like the correct sound even if it is a bit off, but using the word in a sentence helps define the word. People listening will think they heard the word *bigger*, which, in fact, may sound a bit more like *digger*. Practice will improve your skill. You will be able to say "bigger" and say it perfectly.

I have noticed some of the vent courses suggest that you avoid using difficult words in your vent routines, avoiding the hard-to-pronounce letters by using substitution words. For example, instead of the word *bigger*, you could say "larger." That is fine, but if you want to perfect the craft and be impressive as a vent, you need to be able to say the difficult words convincingly and smoothly. Sometimes the best word, say, for a joke or punch line is the more difficult word and gives punch and emphasis to the joke.

There was a very popular ventriloquist in the 1950s, Arthur Worsley, who had a catchphrase using difficult words perfectly. This became his signature bit in his routine. His character would say to the vent, "You can't say it, can you? Go on. Say it. Say, 'A bottle of beer, a bottle of beer.'" He would repeat the phrase over and over very quickly and he always got a huge response from the audience. You will hear a "dottle of deer" the first time you try it, but it will smooth out and become the sound you want. Practice, my friends, practice.

You will see that this is a very tough combination to pronounce well, but if you can perfect that phrase, you are well on your way.

The letter F — This letter is created by using the tongue to replace your lower lip. Say "F" normally. Look in the mirror and notice how your lower lip moves. The lip comes up to meet the bottom of your teeth. The tongue, in this case, does not move in normal speech. However, our method of pronunciation for this letter is using the front of your tongue pressed up against your teeth to get the "fff" sound, which may at first sound like "th." So it goes like "th" and sounds like a lisp. Practice this in front of the mirror, listen to your recorder, and say the letter repeatedly until it sounds correct to you. Do not be afraid to experiment with your tongue placement below the teeth or right behind or at the gum line. Each position alters the sound slightly. Use what feels and sounds best for you.

The letter M — When you hum, you use the "mmm" sound naturally, and your lips are closed. Interestingly enough, a vent has to get this same effect with his mouth slightly open. The letter M begins with the sound "eh," and then add the "mm"—"ehmm." Say the "eh" sound and then push your tongue up against your teeth at the gum line and hum. Together, you will have "ehmm." It will begin to sound like an M. You will at first hear "eng"; that will evolve into the correct sound with practice. The secret lies in the placement of the tongue. The farther forward and flatter the front of your tongue against your teeth, the better the sound will be.

The letter P — This is a very tricky one to get just right. Say it normally moving your lips. Your lips are tightly closed, and then they explode open to get the air sound—"puh." Now add the "ee," and you have "puh-ee." Now run the sounds together to smooth it out, and you get P. The emphasis is on the "ee" sound. If you were to listen to someone shouting from a long distance, you wouldn't hear the "puh" air sound. All you would hear is the "ee." To create the air sound "puh," we have to press the up-curled tip of the tongue behind the teeth, at the gum line, and then blow the sound out. Your tongue will pop forward quickly. With the right pressure behind it, you will get the "puh" sound.

Use your recorder and your mirror with this one when practicing. When you first try it, you will get a sound more like "thee." Once you have got the sound working correctly, a good test of your skill is when you can say, "Peter Piper picked a peck of pickled peppers." Tough one but a good test for you. Practice, practice, and "practice" is a good word to practice on too. You will get it. Just be patient. Remember the tongue placement is critical on this letter. Once you have perfected this vocalization, you will knock their socks off with the Peter Piper bit, but it must be very good.

The letter V — This is a two-part sound—"vvv-eee"—and you use you lower lip against you upper teeth when pronouncing this letter normally. Now use your tongue instead of your lip, place it up behind the teeth at the gum line, make the "vvv" sound, and then add the "eee." It is very easy to slip up on this one. You will find getting the exact sound a bit tricky as the tongue placement is critical for the sound of "vvv." Hold the tongue on the position and say the "vvv" sound. It will tend to sound more like "thee" at first. Keep the "vvv" sound long and try to adjust the tongue position as you are making the sound. You will notice a subtle difference in the sound you are making as you practice the letter. Eventually, it will come to sound more and more like V. Try the phrase "Victor is very valuable." *Valuable* is a tough word, combining the V and B sounds.

The letter W — This letter requires a combination of sounds. It is a three-part letter: "duh-bull-yu." You will need your B-sound skills here to get it right. The "duh" is very natural to form. The "bull" sound is the difficult one to master, and the "yu" is not too much of a stretch. What makes this a difficult letter is the combination of sounds. You have to run them together smoothly to get the letter W—"duh-bull-yu." The first tries will sound like "duggle-yu." Practice with the lips and then without lip movement, comparing the sounds you are getting on your recorder. It will slide into place after a bit of practice. With words like *what*, there is a breath sound; this is "wha-t."

Push the air forcibly out. This is where you breathe, and breathing comes into play.

The letter Y — This is another one of those breathy sounds. The letter sounds like you are saying, "Wuh-eye." The "wuh" sound is difficult, but you will see that you can imitate the sound with the tongue-and-breath combination. It requires a different approach. The position of the tongue is low, thus giving more volume to the mouth. The tongue then curls up as you make the "eye" sound. In addition, you have to push through some air when you pronounce the "wuh" sound.

Note: Just a mention here as an aside. When a ventriloquist first speaks on stage, the audience will scrutinize the act by first focusing on your lip control to see if you move your mouth. If you pass these first few minutes of scrutiny, showing them you are a good ventriloquist, they will then focus on the act, the puppet, and the material. No matter how clever your material or how likeable you and your character are, people will still say, "Loved the puppet. Nice show. But he/she wasn't a very good ventriloquist."

Remember, give them what they want. Be a *good* ventriloquist. That is what you are, and folks want you to succeed. Puppeteers, as in a puppet theatre (e.g., marionettes, hand-puppet operators), are not usually visible to the audience. Therefore, they do not have to worry about lip movement, and of course, the show is usually a monologue. One person or character is speaking to another puppet in the scene. A ventriloquist and his partner are involved in a dialogue, a conversation between two people. Both are visible on stage. Your presentation will come across far more convincing if your technique is flawless. Remember, "of all the best tips, it's frozen lips."

Lesson on the Distant Voices

The ventriloquist's drone and the alphabet have been the main focus of our efforts so far. The distant voice will require a bit more emphasis on the breathing and the development and control of the throat muscles. This technique is truly the primary goal for a competent ventriloquist. Master this, and you will have nailed it! This will increase your performance ability and confidence.

The vocal drone mentioned earlier is the key to the distant voice. This is creating the effect of a voice coming from a distant source. The drone is produced, as mentioned earlier, by tightening the muscles around your vocal chords and throat, holding back the sound and air. Curling you tongue up and back, blocking air and sound, giving a smaller and "tighter" sound—this requires breath control and a tightening-up of the abdominal muscles. The more blocked the sound, the more distant it will seem. By forcing the air out, it gives this effect. This requires extra breath and pressure from your abdomen. This along with closing your mouth a bit more in some cases will give the desired effect.

For example, imagine yourself pushing a heavy object. As you push, you tighten your stomach muscles, squeezing out the air and sound. The voice you hear will be smaller than your puppet's normal speaking voice and have a distant quality. This is the sound you want. The vocal sound produced is also affected by your nasal and cranial (head) cavities. This requires more force when breathing out. The unusual tiny voice has a distinctly distant sound as it resonates through your nasal and cranial (head) cavities. It is not to imply your head has empty space—not completely.

The more the voice is compressed, the more distant it will sound. Consonants are less audible. In a normal voice, for example, when saying, "How are you?" in a distant voice, you would hear more like, "Ow are ooh?" The breath sounds like H in "How are you?" W—as in *what, when,* and *where*—is not an audible vocal sound.

Letter P has a breath sound. This requires practice to learn how to pronounce the letters, words, without using your lips for breath sounds. It is often suggested, as I have mentioned earlier, that you should use substitute letters. For example, for the letter P, use D and make it sound like P or avoid using difficult words altogether. I believe that is not the way to go. The basis of the ventriloquist's technique is to learn how to pronounce the words and letters without substitutions. Instead of using your lips for sounds, you now use your tongue up against the gum line behind your upper teeth and behind your upper lip, which become your new lips if you like.

It takes practice and some time, but as you work with it, you will begin to hear the real sound you are looking for. It does work, believe me. I have heard vents say odd things. For example, for "cowboy boots," it ends up sounding more like "cow-goy goots." Excuse me! It is a good parody on a bad ventriloquist and would get a laugh if used intentionally as part of a funny bit of a really incompetent vent. Unless that is how your act is going to be, the unconvincing ventriloquist can be funny—but not if you are intending it as a proper pronunciation of your material. You get the point. Just be a smooth-talking ventriloquist with a smooth-talking character. It all adds to the believability of your partner. You want people to say, "Wow! Your puppet seems like a real person."

The distant voice requires more practice and patience to perfect. It is the most difficult technique to master. Record your voices as you practice. The thing about distant voices is it requires some distracting of your audience or listener. You would draw their attention to the idea that someone is in a box or outside, on the roof or in the basement or a long distance away from them, or your wristwatch is talking, a bird, whatever you choose as your object or place for the effect.

You focus their attention of this rather than have them looking at you and waiting to hear you "throw your voice."

Like a magician, we use misdirection to fool the audience. Call it vocal magic. As I may have mentioned earlier, it is difficult for us to pin down an exact source of a sound; we need to pay attention to where we believe the sound is coming from. Once you have convinced people to focus away from you, you have the advantage.

The sound of the puppet talking inside the case is a typical routine for the muffled distant voice. You use the small distant voice and block your throat, tighten and restrict it, and using your tongue to block sound and to hold the voice back and breathe in and even close the lips a bit, not completely, you still need the sound to come out. I have to admit that it took me many years to finally perfect a really decent distant voice. I was never too confident that it sounded like a correctly and unmistakably distant-sounding voice. Not until I met Mr. Bergen did I finally understand more about producing the distant voice. He gave me an impromptu lesson during our meeting at the restaurant that got me on the right track and gave me confidence to use the technique. Work with your recording device to practice. You will be your own best critic. You will be amazed that it actually seems to be working when people ask you, "How do you throw your voice?" Just remember to set up the scene, directing people's attention and yours to the place from where the sound should be coming from. Another note: the quality of the distant voice can be altered by the volume in your mouth. Pulling you tongue down, allowing more space in the mouth, changes the sound. Experimenting with this will produce effects that will work well for deeper or higher-pitched sounds.

Breath Control

We need to breathe, and in ventriloquism, the practice is a bit more controlled and pronounced when creating the vocal effects.

Without getting too technical, I will explain what I think are important features of proper breath control in ventriloquism. When producing the ventriloquial voice, your breathing is important to remember. To create the puppet's voice requires you to constrict the sound somewhat and force the breath. Your breathing should be from your stomach. When you do the dummy voice, you will have to force the air up, squeezing your abdomen, putting pressure on the vocal chords, allowing the sound and breath to carry through. The more distant the voice effect, the more restricted your throat muscles and the more force is required to get the breath through. It is sort of like straining when lifting something heavy. You stomach contracts, and you force the air up and out. This is basically the same as the vocal technique used to create the distant voices.

However, with the "near" ventriloquism voice, you need to produce the sound right behind your front teeth, bringing the sound forward as it were. The distant voice is produced farther back and blocked by the tongue to give it a more distant quality. The sound resonates throughout the head and nasal cavity, giving what I call a "head resonance." This, in effect, gives the voice the "hidden" quality, meaning that the listener will find it difficult to determine from where the sound is coming. A strange effect, really, but it does explain the unusual sound quality that this head resonance creates. Hence, a distant voice is the result.

If your lip control is good, people will look right at you while you are making the sound, and they will not know it is you who is speaking or making the sounds. To project your voice effectively, you need to be sure you have a good push of airflow through your vocals. This is important with words that have "breath" sound, like the words *word*, *what*, and *which*, also with the "H" sounds, as in "How are you?" and "Ha!" This is also with the letter Y, for example, and with the letters we call labials—B, M, P, V, and W—which are formed with direct lip control. So having a strong breath push behind the sounds helps get the proper sound out and heard.

I go into more detail with the vocal lessons for the alphabet exercise further on. Each letter has its own sound and method for its creation.

The Puppet's Voice and Character Development

This voice will be your main character voice, the one you will be working with most of the time. Other voices will develop in time, but to begin with, let us work on the main event—your partner.

Depending on the your choice of puppet character, your vocal development of this voice is important. Vents have traditionally gone to a cheeky boy or girl figure. It is the traditional character types you will see working. The voices for these types are generally easier to produce and often are a good contrast from the ventriloquist's voice.

If you have a unique vocal range, a very high-pitched or very low-range voice, this will work for you and give your character an original sound. Pick the vocal range that comes easiest to you. The important thing to remember is to make sure the puppet voice is different from yours. The greater the contrast, the better the effect will be.

If you have an ability to do accents, this will add to your options and material and characters to work with. The accent needs to be different from yours, of course. Consider also the pacing and contrast of voices, your speaking rhythm and inflexion in your speaking style.

I have seen vents whose puppet voice is so much like theirs, it was difficult to tell which one was supposed to be speaking. Record your voices and compare them to your own. There has to be a definite contrast, not only in the pitch but also in the pacing and speech habits and patterns. If you speak slowly and pause a lot between sentences and have a habit of saying something like "um" or some other habit of yours that is typical of your conversational style, then the puppet needs to be different, whatever works to help define your partner character and defines the contrast between you and the puppet.

At this point, the question might be, what comes first—the voice or the puppet? If you have an idea for a character that you want to work with, be sure that you have the vocal range that works for it. I have had characters that I created and could not find the right voice for. That can be a waste of effort and money. So be sure you have the vocal range for the type of puppet you choose. In this matter, I tend to trust my intuition or gut feeling on a character. If you see a puppet that really appeals to you and you have an instant liking for it, you will probably be on the right track. Whichever character voice you decide on, remember that you need to be able to find it easily and be able to sustain it throughout your performance.

For female ventriloquists, creating male voices can be a challenge. This is why you see young boy characters or female characters often used by female vents. Of course, the character you choose needn't be a human. You can have a fantasy character or an animal. Whatever you decide, let it be your own inspiration. I have seen wonderful character ideas in cartoons and film. However, be aware that you cannot outright copy a copyrighted character from a film or publication. You can use them for inspiration, but to take a well-known character—say, for example, Kermit the Frog—and use it as your own will not get you very far in the world of entertainment unless you are doing a tribute show or a promotional event. Try to think long term and be as original as you can. More on this when we talk about where to acquire a puppet, a stock figure or a custom-made one, and what is available in the market today.

I would like to talk about animation, bringing your character to life. Whatever character you choose or type of puppet, we will assume for now that you are using a traditional vent figure. He either sits on your knee or on his own high table or stand, whichever you decide. For this segment, we will assume you are working with a knee- or sitting-type figure.

Today there is a tendency for most vents to work with soft-sculpture figures—for example, the Muppet type of figure. These tend to be more readily available and easier on the budget. Plus, there seems to a be a larger variety of fantasy and animal characters, not like the more traditional knee figure, as we call them, or "hardhead" figures. These tend to be cast from plastic compounds or carved in wood. Wood-carved figures are more expensive and often a lot more difficult to obtain as there aren't as many figure carvers around. Plus, if you are buying an original, created exclusively for you, be prepared to have a pretty long waiting period. It can be as long as a year or more as these puppets are time consuming to produce and often unique one-off creations, a work of art if you like. No two hand-carved figures will be the same, unless they were carved on an automated carving machine—still not going to be that much cheaper to buy. A custom figure can run into a few thousand dollars and more, so go with a stock readymade for now.

Whatever you decide on, it is important that the puppet has a moving mouth. It can be a sock, for that matter, or glove puppet, even a marionette if you like, but the animation of the character and the illusion of the ventriloquist demands a moving mouth—the puppet's, that is, not yours.

While practicing your alphabet, use the puppet. Sit it on your knee or however you want and decide that you and your new partner are going to get acquainted. It helps to suspend reality a little when practicing working with the puppet. This helps define and develop your partner and its relationship with you. This may sound a bit strange to you at first, but remember you are developing an act. You and your figure need to create a team, you the straight man and the puppet the comic or foil.

Synchronizing the puppet's mouth with the words spoken is obviously critical to the illusion. Without proper coordination of the puppet's movement, mouth, and head, your illusion will suffer.

When speaking, the doll's mouth needs to be in time with the words. If you say a word like *hi*, the mouth opens once; if he says *hello*, you will need to open the mouth twice—"hel-lo." Each syllable needs to be expressed with a mouth movement. In some cases, the mouth opens wider for one syllable than another or for a longer period. You can use your own speaking pattern as an example and watch other people's mouths when they speak. The puppet mouth cannot form words as we can, but the flat mouth can effectively seem to form words if you pay attention to the mechanics mentioned above.

For the figure or character—no matter if it is a glove puppet or knee figure—this technique applies. I have seen vents working the figure's mouth so it only opens once for every word no matter how many syllables there are. This looks so uncoordinated and loses a lot of the illusion of the character speaking.

During the dialogue between you and your partner, you need to remember that you are two people speaking to each other, having a conversation. To help understand the dynamics of two people in a conversation, you need to observe this happening. Watch people as they talk to one another. It is interesting to see the different attitudes and reactions each one has to the other person. How is the speaker getting their point across? Is the listener paying attention, is distracted, is bored, thinking of something else? What range of emotions is taking place? These are interesting to consider when you are having a conversation with your partner.

A typical habit many vents have is always looking at the puppet character when it is speaking, a natural enough response, but it can be distracting to your audience. Try to be less concerned about how the puppet is looking while talking. You can practice this in front of a mirror with the figure but not during a performance.

I often look in the opposite direction or at the audience when he is speaking and try to register expressions while being the character. If you are engaged in what is being said and have a reaction to it, the dialogue will appear to sound spontaneous. You do not want to sound like you are reading from a script or sound like you have done this material hundreds of times before. You want to sound fresh and of the moment. You can be either, surprised, smiling, deadpan, dumbfounded, or whatever seems to suit the moment. Try to act focused on what is being said. Look like you are actually hearing this for the first time. This is a natural way for people to respond during conversations. If there is an argument, then obviously, your animated expression adds to the believability of the exchange. Don't be afraid to laugh occasionally when the moment is genuinely funny.

Don't forget the puppet's role in this. These rules apply to it as well. The character needs to express a range of emotions during your dialogue. Consider the character's attitude. Is he/she grumpy, tired, slow, hyper, indifferent, hesitant, confused, scheming, whatever? Keep this in mind. My characters have their own personalities, and each responds differently to me.

I have seen some vents who seem to focus more on what they are saying, using long drawn-out sentences, going on and on about either a story or a setup, all the while the character is sitting, totally still, dead if you like—no movement. Then all of a sudden, it comes to life when it is time for it to speak. This is a bad habit to get into. People are not really that interested in what you have to say. They want to hear the puppet speak, see the interplay between the two characters onstage. Do not neglect the character's animation by it appearing to be playing "dead" while you speak. He needs to be alive, looking, hearing, moving, and responding.

I tend to keep my dialogue moving along, not too many long sentences on my part. I like it to be quick and easy to follow. The setups and punchlines—keep it flowing. My style relies a lot on one-liners, even when it comes to observational humor. Keep the material moving ahead. It is true that a pause onstage seems a lot longer than we think. This can lead to lapses in the continuity and flow of the routine. It's also called comedic timing. Listen to how comics deliver their material. We can learn a lot from some of the greats, not just from ventriloquists. Take a look at other comedic performers. Study their style and delivery. Time the laughs, how many big laughs, say, in one minute. I like to have five good laughs in a minute; more is even better. More on this later in the chapters on performance.

My main characters—Noseworthy, Annie, Bird, the tennis ball, Dennis, and Chester—all have very different voices and personalities, each with their own character traits and movements, giving more life and believability to the illusion of the puppets. A lot of these finer points with the vocal variations will come more easily to you with time and practice. The more you perform, the more you will refine your technique. It took me many years to perfect my main character, Noseworthy. Today his personality is locked in and always comes out convincingly. Experience and repetition is the key to perfection.

The personality of the character is a part of you, your experiences, and people you have known throughout your life. If you have a relative who defines the character you are looking for, don't be afraid to experiment with using those character traits from people you know. This makes for more realism and splits you away from your partner, defines your character more convincingly. The more contrast between you and the character, the better.

My dear uncle Paul was a funny and sarcastic man, very intelligent and most certainly a tease. He was a philosopher, a well-read and well-traveled man. But you never knew when he was serious or just being funny. Difficult man to be around at times. His saving graces were his humility, sense of humour, and empathy for others. I borrowed from his personality to give Noseworthy his edgy attitude.

Writing and Developing Original Material

The choices of material, subject matter, styles, and delivery are endless. There is a wide variety of approaches to writing a script. Collecting jokes and stringing them together in a theme is one way, but then your choice of jokes will probably have been heard before, unless you are clever enough to write your own original stuff.

Before you go into any subject or theme, you will need to consider if your material suits you and your character. As I mentioned earlier, you must first find out who your partner is—his voice, his attitude— and the relationship between the two of you. All this has a bearing on the development of the routines you write. Try to be original as much as you can.

To help you with your first routine, I wrote a bit for a typical smart-aleck type of character, the classic style. The character is putting one over on the ventriloquist, justifying his little swindle by creating lame excuses for his actions. It is a cute bit, and I think you will find it fun to work with.

Suggested Routine

C — Character

V — Ventriloquist

Enter with the doll on your arm. Take your position at the chair or stool with the doll on your knee. You and the character are having an animated discussion as you walk onstage. Your character is in a good mood and very upbeat about something.

V: You sound pretty up today. Why are you in such a good mood? (*pause and look suspiciously at the character*) What have you been up to?

C: Oh yes! It is a good day. Uh-huh, a great day—in fact a fantastic day! (*humming a little tune to himself*) Dee tah da . . .

V: Whenever you are having a really good day, somebody else is having a really bad day.

C: Let's say that I won't be needing any charity from you for a while.

V: Charity? I pay you a weekly salary.

C: Yes, very weakly.

V: Very funny. All right, what have you done, or, should I say, who have you done?

C: Done? Done? You are so suspicious, always expecting the worst. I have made someone very happy, and I made a nice profit doing it.

V: Happy? Doing what? What profit?

C: Well, you know my rich uncle Paul, such a trusting and nice man.

V: Somehow I got the sense that he isn't feeling very nice or trusting after dealings with you. What did you do?

C: I sold him a very nice Rolex watch.

V: Rolex watch? What Rolex? You don't have a Rolex watch.

C: Not anymore, I don't. I had a Rolex—well, a sort of Rolex.

V: Sort of, which means it was a fake.

C: Not really. I would call it a very good-looking replica, a sort of classic reproduction watch type of Rolex—okay, it wasn't real, but he doesn't know it.

V: You sold him a fake!

C: But the five hundred dollars were real. He's happy, I'm happy, we are all happy. Why spoil his fun?

V: Spoil his fun! When he finds out you sold him a fake, he won't be having much fun, and neither will you.

C: Well, you will hide me, right? In the suitcase, right?

V: Forget it, buster. You are going to give him back his money and apologize.

C: He wanted the watch, I wanted the money. I call it a symbiotic relationship.

V: I call it an idiotic relationship, a swindle, a scam! You led him to believe it was real. It will stop working, and when he comes back to you, angry and demanding his money back, you will be in trouble.

C: I'll be in a suitcase. If it stops working, it will have the right time twice a day, right? It has a warranty too, a fifty-fifty warranty, fifty feet or fifty minutes, whichever comes first. (*chuckles to himself*)

V: You are going to give him his money back.

C: All of it? Can I keep a commission?

V: No! You must learn that you can't lie to people. It will lead to dire consequences.

C: Dire? What does that mean?

V: Dreadful, bad, unpleasant, I can give you an example. Have you ever heard the story of Pinocchio?

C: If I say yes, are you still going to tell it to me? Can't say I have. What has that got to do with anything?

V: It is an old Italian fairytale.

C: So why don't you find yourself an old Italian fairy and tell it to him?

V: Once upon a time, there was a woodcarver—his name was Geptepto—who lived in a small village near an enchanted forest.

C: Will this story ever end?

V: Poor Geptepto never had a son, which he always wanted.

C: So he adopted a tree? People adopt highways. Why not trees?

V: Very funny, but you are almost right.

C: Adopted a tree? Sounds a bit like my story.

V: He carved a puppet, a little boy he called Pinocchio, from a magical piece of wood he found in the enchanted forest.

C: Hey, hold on there. You expect me to believe all that?

V: It is a fairy tale. Can I finish the story?

C: Let's do this while we are still young.

V: Now where was I?

C: Lost in the enchanted forest.

V: Geptepto always wanted a son, so he carved a puppet from a magical piece of wood he found in the enchanted forest, which he called Pinocchio.

C: Say, I was thinking—so who were my parents?

V: Look, I am telling a story here. Do you mind?

C: Okay, but I was wondering who my parents were.

V: You don't have any parents. May I continue?

C: What do you mean? Of course I do.

V: I created you. You don't exist. You're a figment of my imagination. Now may I continue with the story?

C: Oh, really? If you created me, I made you!

V: Getting back to the story, Geppetto carved a puppet from a magical piece of wood that he found in the enchanted forest.

C: So where is all this leading to?

V: When Pinocchio told a lie, his nose would grow longer.

C: I've already heard it. So who were my parents?

V: We are out of time.

C: Time? Say, how would you like to buy a watch?

Exit.

(This is a suggestion for a routine you might like to work with.)

Chapter Five

Character Design

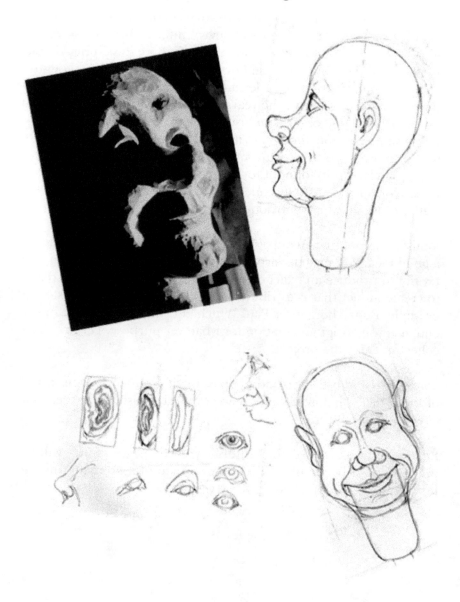

Choose Your Partner

There are endless choices for character types. I am talking more about human characters, not fantasy or animal, if that is your choice, but for our purpose here, the carving process shown is devoted exclusively to human-type puppets.

I usually create a number of drawings to help me develop my character ideas. I have included a few of my sketches to give you an idea of personality types. You may, of course, have something already in mind—the traditional little boy, old man, or lady. A male figure is most common and what I learned to build. Female characters, I have created several over the years. If you have a picture of one you like, work with that or even an inspiration of a person you may know. Either way, give some thought to it. I have built puppets that I thought would be great to work with and ultimately found out that I just couldn't relate to it, found it too difficult to find a voice or material to develop an act. I usually ended up selling it or, in some cases, even trading with another ventriloquist.

I must point out that an outright copy of someone else's puppet is not a good idea. You may be inspired by a character you have seen, but try not to produce an exact copy, unless, of course, you are looking to create an act that is a tribute to a well-known ventriloquist—for example, Edgar Bergen or Paul Winchell from the past. But in the end, it is your original creation for whatever purpose. Performer or collector, enjoy the project.

Some ventriloquists have had puppets made in their likeness, a sort of "mini-me." That is fun and an idea you may wish to pursue, your alter-ego kind of thing.

Remember, you are creating an original work of art, and it will be unique and only one of its kind, so be proud of it no matter how it turns out. You will improve as you try again.

Arthur—I built him for Mark Wade. He has a very similar
likeness to my Noseworthy character. The original Arthur is
now living in the Vent Haven Museum of Ventriloquism in
Kentucky. Mark works with a duplicate figure of Arthur.

Leprechaun I built for Peter Rolston, a local artist who had a kids'
television show.

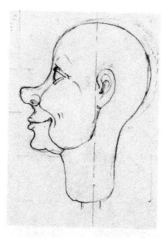

Profile study of a young boy character, what I would call a generic puppet type, typical of the kind of figures many of the early ventriloquists preferred, and still very popular today.

Sketches I was working on, looking for an idea for a very specific character type.

The hockey character I eventually built, Jacques Le Strapp. He is now in the collection of the brilliant figure maker Tim Sellburg.

Here is Murray, a true-to-life creation I made back in 1984. He was inspired by a friend of mine who worked for this guy in real life, a local investor and businessman who never took a liking to this guy. Murray now lives in a private collection, unemployed.

Be an Original

To develop an original character and act, we will be influenced by those before us. They define where the art of vent is and where it is heading. Innovations, original ideas, and fresh new approaches can still be created. Talent is a part of the equation, but hard work is most of it. You have to put in the work and time to perfect the craft, become a good technician and animator. Watch as many performers as you can. Learn from those who have gone before you. Most professional vents working today began when they were young.

I started my journey when I was eleven years old, listening to the Edgar Bergen and Charlie McCarthy show on the radio, reading a book from the school library, and watching Paul Winchell's early television shows in the '50s. I started by imitating other vents and then eventually found my own style and material. It was a long process, a period of many years, before I could lay claim to my own act and original innovations. My biggest motivation was the building of the puppets, at least in the beginning. I wanted to have the perfect puppet partner, and not until I met Pop Steinman—who taught me how to build, carve, and animate—did I begin to achieve that goal.

It was many years later before I had enough experience to create an original act. I used many innovations, some inspired by Steinman, others I developed myself. The simple idea of having the doll stand on his own feet, with a rod attached to his left arm, the figure standing on his own table, was a new idea. No other vent I knew had ever worked that way except Pop. He had devised these features and more in his characters. Eventually, I learned to build these mechanics myself.

Edgar Bergen passed away in Las Vegas in 1975. Prior to his passing, he was making a bit of a comeback, but unfortunately, his heart gave out that evening after his first night at the Flamingo Hotel. Bergen was a great pioneer in the art and inspired many of the vents whom you see today, including myself. His three characters—Charlie, Mortimer, and Effie—were assigned to a friend of the family for refurbishing to become a permanent exhibit at the Smithsonian Institute, where they reside today.

As it turned out, I was in Los Angeles, visiting with my friend who was involved with the restoration work on the dolls. I was able to handle and see the puppets up close and personal. That was a huge thrill for me at the time, and I learned a lot about the finer points of these famous characters, which I had watched on television, heard on the radio, and seen in pictures in various publications on ventriloquism over the years. Shortly after this time, reproductions of these famous puppets started to turn up and were offered for sale. There is a mystery surrounding just how many originals there were. At one point, it was claimed by this individual that there were, in fact, ten duplicates in existence, and most could be purchased through this person for a very hefty price. In reality, there were probably only two or three copies of the originals. Somebody was cashing in on the Bergen creations.

The Early Years

This is the evolution of a young aspiring ventriloquist and the beginnings of what became a fifty-year-plus career. When we are young and impressionable, we see the future as a time we can only imagine, let alone what we might be doing in that future. At eleven years old, I thought the future was going to be robots, space travel, and flying people and cars, maybe even having a job as a ventriloquist. That was a dream for me. It eventually came to be just that. I had a vivid imagination and was fascinated with anything new that looked like what the high-tech future might be like. *High-tech*? Not a word in our vocabulary back then. I was very interested in robotics, and that is partly how I became absorbed in learning how to build a robot. We didn't have the technology we have today. But that interest wound its way into puppetry. The closest I came to building a robot was a ventriloquist's puppet.

Some character sketches for the hockey guy. The carved head in progress and the final finished version.

Computers were not even on the radar. In fact, radar was a relatively new and amazing invention itself. I never dared to consider that I could be professional ventriloquist. It was another fascinating hobby for me that grew over the years.

Ms. Edith, an interesting idea, which was inspired by my mother,
Edith. There is a strong resemblance.

I first came across ventriloquism listening to Edgar Bergen on the radio and then watching Paul Winchell on television in the '50s and '60s, the ever-popular Sunday-night *Ed Sullivan Show,* where ventriloquists would turn up quite often. I saw Bergen, Winchell, Senior Wences, Sammy King, Arthur Worsley from England, and many others over those early years of television.

I had no idea how ventriloquism was done, but I knew that was what I wanted to learn. Fate played a hand in my good fortune when a friend of mine, Eugene, a kid in my grade-seven class, showed me a book he found at the school library on ventriloquism. It was an old English publication on ventriloquism with instructions and pictures. That started me off. The belief that one day I would become a ventriloquist never left me.

After my initial attempt at building a puppet, the first Clarence, I met Pop Steinman in a toy shop in Vancouver. That was Christmas 1953. Aaron Miller, a.k.a. Pop Steinman, who was a master carver and figure builder—he taught me the craft of carving puppets.

The whole idea of building my own puppet never ceased to fascinate me. When I was fourteen, we lived in Penticton, a small town in British Columbia, Canada. By this time, I had completed my first carved puppet under the critical eyes of my friend and tutor, Pop Steinman. That was Clarence number two. I was performing a few shows for friends and family and my classmates. The first time I performed for money, I received a fee of five dollars and was thrilled being paid for something I loved to do. I could not believe that someone was going to pay me to play a ventriloquist. I wasn't really sure if I was even doing it right.

I still remember the excitement I experienced on that evening. I heard the band play that last number before I was introduced, the bass drum thumping. I wasn't sure if it was my heart about to jump out of my chest or the beat of the drum. I was "pumped," as we say today. It went off fine. Even though the routine was very juvenile, written for children, it was one of the routines Paul Winchell had in his book (the only routine I had then). I received a big round of applause plus a fee of five dollars and a write-up in the local newspaper, the *Penticton Herald*. My first press write-up—that was 1955.

Being a shy kid, to create a response of laughter and applause from adults was almost overwhelming for me. It was a revelation to use my puppet creation to speak for me. This gave me the attention and praise for something that I was so intensely interested in. I was becoming clever in performing but only in a stage setting. Otherwise, I was very shy about drawing attention to myself, especially among my peers.

As a twelve-year-old kid in grade school, I was a loner. The few friends I had, most of who were a bit on the nerdy side, were not what you call popular or one of the in-crowd kids. Neither was I. I was very awkward around the gatherings of the popular students. I would walk past a group of kids by crossing the street to avoid passing them on the same side. Donny Bryan was not an academic. I had to struggle with the three Rs. I did, however, excel in wood and metal shop work and the visual arts of drawing and sculpting. I enjoyed making things, creating projects, living out my childhood fantasies through my projects and creations.

My childhood heroes were Superman, Roy Rogers, Batman, Tarzan, and, of course, Edgar Bergen and, in time, Paul Winchell. My projects included a Superman costume, Indian stuff (bows and arrows), and knights in armour. I was fascinated with the story of King Arthur and the knights of the round table. Naturally, I had to have a suit of armour, so I built three complete suits, with visored helmets and all. My friends and I would joust with lances on our bicycles in the alley behind my house, a bit dangerous—a wonder no one got hurt. My other fascination was Tarzan. He had gorillas, so I wanted a gorilla costume too. I built a very realistic gorilla costume and would scare the kids in my neighbourhood whenever I ventured out in my costume. Man, was I a weird kid or what?

Astronomy become another fascination, along with spaceships and aliens. I made an alien costume, very nice, and then started building a large telescope. It never was completed; I couldn't afford the cost of some of the parts that I needed. I then decided I wanted to be like

Elvis and took up the guitar around the time Elvis was starting to make a hit. I had the Elvis hair but not the voice. I played my guitar and had fun with my buddies in our folk-singing garage band.

After all these projects, ventriloquism remained a constant interest and stayed with me. I was trying to build my first dummy in 1952, and with the help and guidance from my new friend, a brilliant figure carver, Mr. Aaron "Pop" Steinman, eventually, I became a competent figure maker and amateur ventriloquist.

There is a lot to be said growing up in an era without television. Later in the '50s, we acquire a television. No computers, MP3 players, CD or DVD players, flash drives, computers, or cell phones. Nowadays we have an endless array of electronic and entertainment devices that are available at reasonable prices. I think the absence of these technologies during my early years allowed me to focus on my varied interests and quirky fascination with all things mechanical and play out my fantasies by creating and building.

In my early school days, the family moved around a lot, living in small towns all over British Columbia—Victoria, Lac la Hache, Hundred Mile House, Vancouver, and Penticton B.C. I had to create my own toys and projects. I was not an athletic kid, so baseball, hockey, and football were activities that did not interest me that much. I did get into chess.

Later in high school, I signed on to the football squad. I had to as my best friend Bill was a star and talented player on the team at North Vancouver High School. To become more effective as a defensive lineman, I needed to get bigger and stronger, so it was then that I got into weight training. I wanted to look like Superman or Tarzan and wanted to be big and powerful, a fearsome tackle on the defensive high-school football team. The shy kid was coming out of his shell by then. In the later years, I became intensely interested in bicycle racing, but that was in the early seventies and another story that occupied nine years of my life.

I am getting a bit off the track and ahead of myself, but these activities and interests occupied my life and time as a kid. I am grateful that I had very tolerant and liberal parents during the juvenile and school periods of my life. I was always into some new activity or hobby. However, with all these interests, my academic talent was never that impressive. I have to say I loved books.

Family portrait—my sister Lisa and I with our parents Edith and Gaylord Bryan in London just after the war in 1945. We immigrated to Vancouver, Canada, the following year.

I have learned a lot through my various interests and developed a taste for travel. I wanted to see the world and all the different cultures. This still interests me to this day. Luckily, as a performer on cruise ships, I have been able to accomplish my dreams of travel and work as a professional ventriloquist.

My first carved Clarence. Boy, was I proud of this character.
I built him with the guidance of my friend Pop Steinman.
Four years later, I built my second Clarence.

Our family emigrated from England just after the war in 1946. Our
home was Vancouver, British Columbia. This is where I have lived till
today. My father Gaylord Ernest Bryan's family came from Ireland.
My dad was born in England. He was a journeyman fitter, painter,
and all-around handyman. His real career, however, was an actor on
the London stage and film. He also worked as a stuntman, wrangling
and training horses.

He was an artist and had the temperament of one, a man's man if you
like. We immigrated to Canada, and our dad, always up for a good
rollicking adventure and new business opportunity, moved us all over
the province. As result of that wanderlust, our family was shuttled
around. My sister and I were in and out of different schools, on the

average of one a year, until we entered high school. I graduated from North Vancouver High in 1963.

Dad never did get back into theater and was attempting a variety of business ventures that, unfortunately, never did pan out. It ended up that our mother had to work and became the main breadwinner in the family, much to Dad's frustration. Money was always scarce in those years and added to my father's deep depression. Dad always said if he had to, he would wash floors for Mom. Eventually, he did just that.

Our mother, Edith, came from a well to-do European family. Her mother died when she was very young, and her father, a very successful businessperson in London and Vienna, made sure that his beautiful daughter was well taken care of. Our mother, Edith Maria Sonntag, was living a very privileged life, traveling Europe, with fine clothes, high-society friends, and expensive holidays in the Alps. Things changed after the war when she met our father and moved to the new world, Canada, and they began their adventures with the family. We lived on farms and ranches, hobby farms of the wealthy, where Dad was the groundskeeper and horse trainer. Mom became the house matron, planned and cooked for the lavish parties for the visiting guests and dignitaries.

These were great times for us kids. My sister and I became very accomplished horse riders through the instruction and training from our dad, the equestrian/cowboy. Eventually, we ended up in Vancouver and stayed put. Our father was also a very gifted artist and painted wonderful images. My sister and I picked up this interest and artistic trait as well. My sister, Lisa, to this day, makes her living as an artist and art publisher in Carmel, California. My talents veered off into other directions, where I eventually became a performing ventriloquist with my hand-carved puppets.

This brings me back to today and this book on ventriloquism. The stories of my family would fill many chapters, but for this purpose, the early history of my family serves to give a bit of background, the telling of how events, places, and people I have known through the years have shaped my character and my professional career as a ventriloquist.

Being the traditionalist I am, I have kept this book focused on a style of ventriloquism that has been recognized as a sort of standard for me, greatly influenced by Edgar Bergen. Bergen so impressed me when I was younger, and still to this day, I find I can learn from his style and technique. His performing style was always natural, conversational, and fun to watch. I guess I have always wanted to emulate this and have evolved over the years into my own way of interpreting this classic and seemingly effortless showmanship that Bergen was a master of. His performances were enjoyed by all ages. Even today I find I can still learn from watching his shows. Dated as the material is, it still holds a lot of appeal and ideas. I wanted to bring that charm and easy style into my performances.

The art of performing ventriloquism using a knee figure is the traditional approach. I have explored and worked this style in this book, hoping to pass on to you what I have learned. There are many innovators in the field. Keep in mind that there are still possibilities and opportunities for original interpretation, limited only by your imagination.

As you can see, my appearance and that of my characters has changed considerably. It seems I didn't have much choice in the change of my appearance as I got older. Both myself and the character seemed to have aged. How's that happened? There is an evolution taking place. Both the artist and the act have matured, and that is what we have to remember—if you aren't changing, you aren't moving ahead. Everything changes. Nothing stays the same. That is how we grow to our full potential. I have always believed that we never stop learning and keep recreating ourselves, aspiring to be more by exploring new ideas. Don't be afraid of failure. That is how we learn.

I had plenty of failed projects, ideas that were just not practical or doable with my resources and the family's agenda. As I said, we moved a lot during those early times. My sister and I attended more than nine different schools before we graduated from North Vancouver High School in 1959. The Bryan family was always on the move as a result of my mother and father's work commitments.

Design and Build Your Own Character

The following is a detailed description of the process. I should mention that this is a big project and requires a number of woodworking tools and materials. Each section's front and back pieces are then finished separately and hollowed out. The access trap door is fashioned separately.

My preferred method is a traditional approach to the figure-carving techniques that I was taught by a master carver. I was very lucky to have the opportunity to be given firsthand teaching and hands-on methods many years ago, and I have continued to use the methods I was shown back then by my friend and teacher, Mr. Steinman.

This project is not for everyone, but if you think you can manage, give it a try. I have attempted to provide as much detail as possible. It is a very rewarding pursuit and worth the effort. I have found that I prefer to work with my own creations. They all have something of me in them that makes the character more relevant to me in the process.

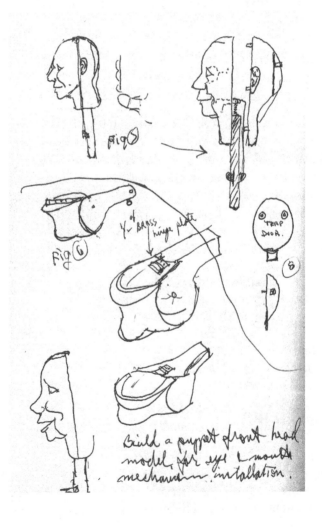

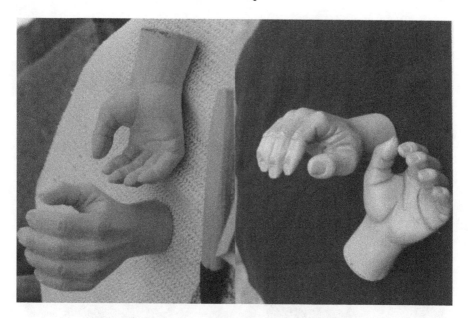

Carved hands, fitted on Noseworthy character.

Photo with my current cast of characters, Noseworthy, Miss
Annie, (soon to be replaced with Miss Dottie Potts,) The Bird
and Chester Fields, a creation of Tim Selberg of Selberg Studio.

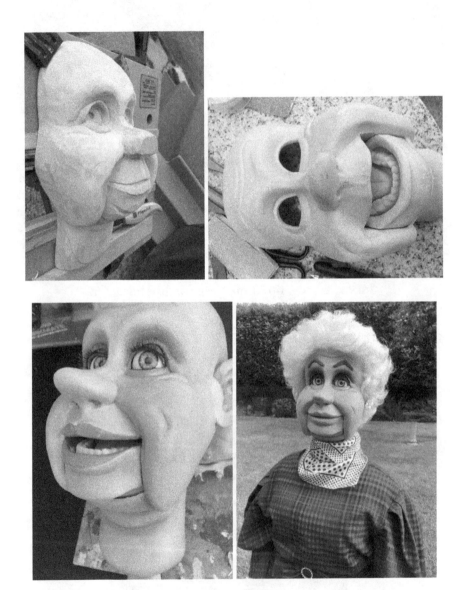

Here is a series of photos showing the development
of new character dottie potts

Creating and Carving Your Puppet Partner

Here is my latest creation still in progress, Miss Dottie
Pots. She will be a red head with some down home
values and a foil for the outspoken Mr. Noseworthy.

Carving Methods, Tools, and Tips

Details of Figure Construction

1. Carving Process:

- Head Details

- Hand and Body Details

- Painting, Hair, and Wardrobe

- Finishing and Mechanics

Let me start by saying this—you do not have to build your own puppet to become a ventriloquist. I guess that is obvious, but I felt I should bring it up. Figures are available from a number of very talented builders whom you can find online these days. I will list a few for your interest later toward the end of this segment.

It is interesting to note, for example, that in the tradition of the native carvers in the Northwest Coast of Canada and the United States who are recognized as some of the best in the world have a strict apprenticing tradition. The master would apprentice the novice carver by first teaching him to make his own carving tools. Then he would learn the art forms and the mythology of their religious symbols, their tribal ceremonies and traditions. Their incredible totem poles interpreted the family and tribal history. The beautifully carved masks represent their mythological characters and are used, even to this day, in dances and ceremonies. These remarkable works of art are sacred to their beliefs and native culture. The student would apprentice under a master carver for some years before being considered worthy and skilled enough to be recognized as a carver within their clan.

This too is the practice of the *bunraku* puppeteers in Japan, the ritualized traditional puppet theater of Japanese culture. Theirs is a highly formalized theatrical art form. The novice puppeteer was taught the formalities of the craft from the bottom up through the master carver and often the principal puppet operator. He was the teacher, your sensei.

It is a Zen-like form of study and training, involving ancient practices, following traditional formalities of indoctrination into the guild of the puppet theatre. It is actually an opera. The student has to learn the traditional stories and songs involved in the storyline of the plays. It was more a school of theatre rather than puppetry; in fact, it is an opera performed with traditional characters from Japanese folklore.

In some ways, the art of creating and carving ventriloquist dummies is a lost art and is learned usually by apprenticing or at least working with a figure maker. Unfortunately, that is not always possible. There are very few builders available for personal instruction. The alternative is to learn from a book or video. The personal touch whereby one learns the craft from a master just is not practical for most people these days. I will do my best within my book to pass on the craft of figure carving as I have learned throughout the years.

Luckily, aspiring ventriloquists today do not have to build their characters, make their tools, or join a religious or cultural group, purchasing their figures either from a magic shop or, if lucky enough, directly from the figure maker. You can now go online and look up ventriloquist dummy builders or carvers, and you will find a number whom you may contact and commission to build a character.

If you order a "stock character," these are less expensive and more available. What we call stock figures, reproductions, are mass-produced from moulded duplicates, not one-off originals. You will pay a lot more for an original figure. Stock figures are available for around the five-hundred-dollar range or more, depending on the complications of movements and detailing. Professionals and collectors alike will spend a lot more, paying upward from a couple of thousand dollars to over ten thousand for a custom-made, hand-carved figure, featuring a variety of animations and movements, some even with electronics. It can take a quality figure maker months to complete a made-to-order figure, created either in a plastic compound or wood, and often you are on a waiting list for up to two years.

Having said that, you will get a lot of satisfaction creating your own partner, and certainly, it will be a lot cheaper in dollars but not in the time invested. Of course, there is eBay, a good place to check out for used and antique figures, which become available from time to time. You may have considered that option before you bought this book.

Building a ventriloquist's puppet is a challenging project, at least the way I like to do it. This is not a fast and easy project; I follow traditional methods of figure building involving woodcarving. Papier-mâché is a traditional method too but not as permanent or durable as wood. I will not get into papier-mâché construction in this book. Woodcarving was how most of the traditional figures were created in the time of Bergen and Paul Winchell up until the arrival of synthetic materials, fibreglass, plastics, latex rubber, and a variety of compounds available today. So wood it is for this project.

This project requires some ability for working in wood or at least some experience with carving using a variety of woodworking tools. You will need a workshop environment or at least a place where you can make some mess and a bit of noise. Even if you haven't been working with woodcarving or cabinet building, you can, with patience and determination, learn this fascinating craft.

When I was eleven years old and smitten with the whole ventriloquism mystique, the first thing I had to have was a real ventriloquist puppet, not a toy. I worked from a book I found at the school library as my inspiration, containing many pictures of vent puppets and, of course, my idol, Edgar Bergen's Charlie McCarthy. I began or attempted to build a vent figure from a moulding compound of flour, water, and asbestos powder, a product we were using in art class in my school back in the '50s. Asbestos powder—can you imagine? This is a very dangerous product if inhaled and is all but banned today!

My first creation was not a thing of beauty. I called him Clarence. It was cumbersome, heavy, and only lasted for one performance before it self-destructed when it fell from its perch on a stool—a big disappointment, you can imagine. From that point on, I was more determined than ever to try to carve a figure. I had to have a *real* wooden puppet.

Paul Winchell was the current major ventriloquist in 1955. He had his own television show and published a book, *Ventriloquism for Fun and Profit*, with a section on carving or using papier-mâché to build a vent doll. I struggled with this instruction and found it to be too simplistic and lacking detail in its concept. I was not getting anywhere fast either with my block of wood and my tools, which were woefully inadequate. I learned through trial and error that there was a whole lot more to hand-carving a figure than this book provided.

By a stroke of luck, I met my personal instructor (who became my sensei) and later my friend, Pop Steinman, who lived in Vancouver. He was an amazing carver of ventriloquist dummies. Only then did I make some progress and learned how to carve and design my own vent figure. Eventually, I became quite good at this, and some years later, I was creating figures for other vents.

I do not build custom figures these days. I am too busy working as a professional performer, traveling extensively, which is what a working act does. Perhaps one day I will again sit down in my workshop and create characters. However, now I am not able to embark on that project. When that day does arrive, I will make it known through my website, Donbryan.com, and that of the ventriloquists' association, Venthaven.com, that Don Bryan–crafted figures are once again available. In the meantime, through this book, I want to pass on what I have learned and enjoyed over the years and hope to inspire you to develop your skills as a competent ventriloquist and figure maker.

If I have not scared you off at this point and you still feel you want to take on this fascinating project, shall we get started? I will begin by going over the tools and materials required.

Shop and Tool Items

You will find most of the tools you require in the professional woodcarving outlets. They offer everything you need in hand tools, including the basswood for the head and hands. See the references for outlets. In Canada, Lee Valley Tools and Canadian Tire stores are excellent for hand-tool resources. They have shops all across Canada. In the United States, you can find similar shops specializing in woodcarving and crafter's supplies. Home Depot's tools department is a very good place to search out many shop items.

Workbench

Your carving area should be a solid workbench. You will need a woodworking and metalworking vice and a selection of clamps used for gluing and holding work pieces. You can build your own bench from two-by-fours and three-quarter-inch plywood or look for a readymade model with a built-in woodworking vice. These are available at the specialty woodcrafters' supply stores and occasionally at Costco or larger hardware supply stores with a good selection of tools. I have seen great benches at IKEA on occasion. Also in Canada, Lee Valley Tools has a great selection of woodworking benches and carving tools.

I have found carving with a bench stop is very handy, allowing you to work your piece on the bench without it sliding around. You can build your own bench stop as shown. You should also have an apron made of a heavy material, canvas or leather. When working your pieces on your lap, it protects you from slips with the edge tools. Another very helpful item is a perforated rubber mat called a carver's pad or mat. This product can be found in carving supply shops. As a substitute, you can use a similar type of mat used as a shelf liner. The mat is used on the bench top to help keep you work piece from moving around while carving.

Interesting female character I was commissioned to build for a vent in New York back in 1975.

Power Tools

- A full-size band saw is ideal. However, if you don't have access to this, you can work with handsaws, the type used in cabinetry work (see notes below).

- Power Dremel (optional) or rotary tool — This handy device comes usually in a kit, with a selection of bits, drills, and cutting and polishing attachments. Use for fine detail and smoothing cuts in wood or metal. This item is a luxury and not necessary. All work of this type can be done with hand tools.

- A cordless power drill — This comes with a selection of bits, including some paddle bits, smaller up to a quarter inch, a half inch, three quarter inches, and an inch.

- Soldering iron — This is a solder used for brass rods and wires.

List of Hand Tools

Chisels and gouges are varied in their selection. I recommend the following for this project. You have the option of using fewer tools; this all depends on your level of skill and experience with carving and woodworking.

- Gouge sizes: three quarter inches, a half inch, or a quarter-inch scoop

- Gouge (V shape): a half inch, a quarter inch

- Firmer flat: three quarter inches, a quarter inch

- Spoon gouge: a half inch

These are suggestions if you have access to Lee Valley Tools Ltd. Canada or, in Oregon, Sugar Pine Woodcarving Supplies. There are numerous others throughout the United States. Most carry a wide variety of woodcarving tools and specialty items plus a stock of carving woods. Their staff are very knowledgeable and can offer advice, tips, and resources for woodcarvers. I noticed there are a number of outlets around the country for woodcarvers' supplies. Just go online and ask Google; she seems to know everything.

In addition to chisels, you will need to have a good-quality short-blade carving knife. Not a pocket knife—you need a short fixed blade with a long handle, a whetstone for sharpening your chisels, some fine oil to surface the stone, and small curved stones for the gouges and scoop-shaped blades. You will need a selection of coarse- and fine-grain sandpaper. Also very useful is black sandpaper for metal smoothing, which helps with chisel sharpening.

- Saws—handsaw, backbone saw or Japanese pull saw, hacksaw, copping saw

- A selection of files, fine- to course-rasp wood files, metal file (a set of jeweller's files are handy but not vital)

- Woodcarving mallet

One of the most useful machines to have in your workshop is a band saw. I have one large and a smaller unit for fine work—not really necessary but makes for quicker work—but you can still get that done with a small handsaw. You will need a soldering iron kit with solder for the brass rods and tubes.

- Sculptor's callipers, double ended

- Staple gun (use quarter-inch, half-inch, and three-eights-inch staples)

- A variety of sand papers, from coarse to fine, for metal and wood

- Adhesives—white wood glue and contact cement (the "buttery" kind, easy to spread and work with); superglue (a very fast-drying product and comes under the name Zip or Flash. Use the medium consistency. This is available in hobby shops); wood putty (Elmer's is one product I use for filling small cracks and holes, also used for filling in carving mistakes. This is an all-round handy product to help with the detailing and finishing work)

There are also some very useful products that are a putty type; they usually come in two segments. What I find extremely useful is Bond-Aide. One part is an activator and sets up very quickly once you have kneaded the two parts together. Great for filling and even creating small parts. It hardens into a strong and durable product that can be carved, shaped, and painted. You can also press the putty into a small mould to create duplicate items and use it to create a small mould as well.

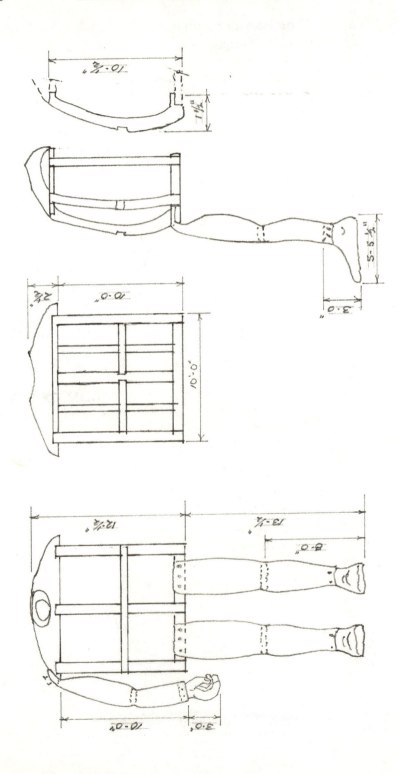

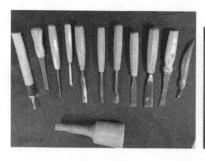 

Woodcarving tools with a mallet. These are some
of the chisels and knives I work with.
Bench stop for a carving base—stops movement
of your material—and headrest cradle.

Carving Woods

The preferred carving wood for the head and hands is basswood.
This is a light softwood, more common to the southeastern part
of North America. Do not consider balsa wood as an alternative;
it is way too soft. You should be able to find basswood in specialty
wood supply shops and carvers outlet stores. Lee Valley Tools carries
specialty carving woods of all kinds. I have used red cedar and yellow
cedar when I could not find basswood. These other alternatives are
not ideal. Red cedar, the more common, is a good carving wood;
however, the grain can be very wavy and difficult to cover, and it
tends to splinter. Yellow cedar is quite hard to work, heavier, and not
recommended. Having said that, it is a very strong alternative to red
cedar and does come out very well for carving, just a bit harder to
work with and, as I said, heavier. Carving wood needs to be dry, not
green. Interestingly, however, most indigenous Indian carvers prefer
to work their larger carvings in green wood that has not been kiln
dried. I don't recommend it for our purpose.

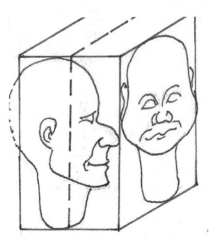

DRAW PROFILES
ON GLUED HALVES.

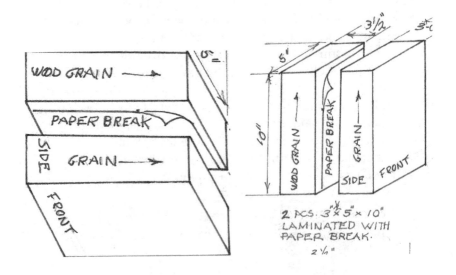

WOOD GRAIN →

PAPER BREAK

SIDE

GRAIN →

FRONT

6" =

3½"

3" =

5"

10"

WOOD GRAIN

PAPER BREAK

GRAIN

SIDE

FRONT

2 PCS. 3"½" × 5" × 10"
LAMINATED WITH
PAPER BREAK.
2 ½ "

For the head, you will need two pieces of basswood, five by three by ten inches. Select wood with a fine straight grain and no knots. If you can find this in a five-by-four-by-ten piece, this is even better. For the hands, you will need two pieces of basswood, three by two by six inches. For the ears, the back-of-the-head trap door, jaw, and feet, you need two pieces of 2x4x10 and two 1x1x12.

- Canvas for arms and legs, body covering (medium weight; two yards of material)

- Two ping-pong balls, white, for eyes

- Plastic or glass irises for the eyes (check out the craft shops for these. I have used taxidermist eyes, but it is difficult to find a human-looking eye for obvious reasons)

- One-and-one-quarter-by-twelve-inch wood doweling for head stick; a one-by-one-by-twelve-inch square will work as well

- Brass tubing and rods used for controls and movement mechanisms (These items are available from model building supply or hobby stores. Refer to section on eye and mouth movements for details.)

- Light expansion springs for mouth and eye return mechanisms

- A selection of brass screws, small nuts, bolts, and washers

- Paints (I prefer to use oil-based artist's colors. However, acrylic paints will do fine. They are water soluble and readily available)

Painting

The paint and brushes are available from arts supply hobby and craft stores. The artist's oil colors you need are white, burnt sienna, light red, Payne's gray, light yellow, and black. Buy small tubes of paint; you won't need much of it for the mix. I use a small glass jar, say, like a jam jar.

Pour a small amount of white undercoat paint and add a small ribbon of burnt sienna and light red, raw umber, a smaller amount. Mix together in the jar to create a flesh tone, adding a bit of color or more white to get the right tone. I also use a very small amount of light yellow in the mix. After the mix is well blended, take a small amount of paint and pour onto a glass or plastic plate and continue to blend with a brush. When you have the right color, apply with a brush to the head. You can modify the color if need be. I like to use some extra reddish tones on the cheeks and ears for contrast. Around the eyes, I darken the paint a bit for shading and outline the eyelids like a mascara. You can paint on the eyebrows or, like I do, create them with some hair from a paintbrush or cutting from the wig. I cut a paper pattern and stick the hair onto it. When dry, trim and apply to the head.

With oils, I use a flat white undercoat as a base and mixing medium for the colors. Oils take longer to dry but are very durable, retaining their color and luster for many years. You will need turpentine or paint thinner as a medium for the oils and, of course, some rags and mixing palettes. I premix the flesh tone in a small container, which I can seal after I am done, and have a small amount left over for touch-up paint and the hands. The brushes I use are artist quality, three or four; the sizes range from about half-inch to fine pointed hairbrushes for fine detailing around the eyes and mouth.

For the final finishing coat on your head and hands, you could use a clear or matte non-shine spray-on lacquer. This protects the finish and keeps the paint from becoming worn or shiny over time. If you use artist oils, you probably won't need to use a clear coat. After many years of use, none of my finishes have deteriorated or become shiny. If the character has facial lines, as on an older character, blend some paint from your flesh tone to make it a bit darker for the creases. I usually let the paint dry till it gets a bit tacky, and then I use a natural sea sponge. They are very porous and dab the paint all over the head. This adds some skin texture to the finish and helps eliminate shiny spots, a more natural finish. The sponge also helps when blending the shading of colors.

For hair or wigs, you may want to wait before you purchase this as you may have changed your ideas about hairstyles by the time you have finished the head and have a better sense of the character.

Eyelashes are available from the makeup department in a drugstore. You will find a large variety from which to choose. Most eyelash sets designed for women tend to be too long, but you can cut them down to work for a male character. Attach them with superglue on top of the eyelid. Be careful not to spill any glue on the puppet's eyes. If you install the lashes on the inside of the lid, do that before you install the eyes. I have used light kid-glove leather for eyelids. This allows for a very close fit of the eyelids over the eyeballs. While you are in the makeup department, you should pick up some clear nail polish for the figure's fingernails. If your character is a female, you may want to choose a coloured polish.

I have believed in the details. They are important to the overall character design and add subtle lifelike reality to a character.

I built this guy back in 1974 and sold it to a ventriloquist in New York. Interesting that he turns up here for sale at the VENTRILOQUIST CONVENTION for ten times more than what I sold it for. One of my best pieces of work.

Front Head Profile on Block

When laying out your design, use a large sheet of paper and draw the head profiles in full scale. Based on your wood block, use dimensions of 5x6x10 inches. You will need a front, side, and rear view of the head. Refer to the figure drawing. Be sure to align the main features across the page. Draw guidelines as shown, along with a centre line for the front view. The opposing views need to correspond where the eyes, nose, mouth, and ears are located.

The dimensions I have shown on the figure drawing are a guide as your dimensions will vary from my mine, dependent on the design. A mirror is a handy guide for checking your drawing for balance and symmetry so that both sides of the facial features are properly aligned. The reflection will show up flaws and imbalances in the features. In a human face, it is a fact that when you divide the face on a center line, top to bottom, and compare sides, they will differ. Perfectly balanced faces are rare. It is these imbalances that give a face character.

Despite variations, it is, however, important to try and make the face realistic and appear correct. Eyes are on the same line, nose is in the center of the face, the ears are at the same height and size—you get the idea. Too-perfect puppet faces look unnatural and "puppet like."

Drawing of front on block of basswood, five inches wide, three inches thick, twelve inches tall, and carved version before the nose is extended.

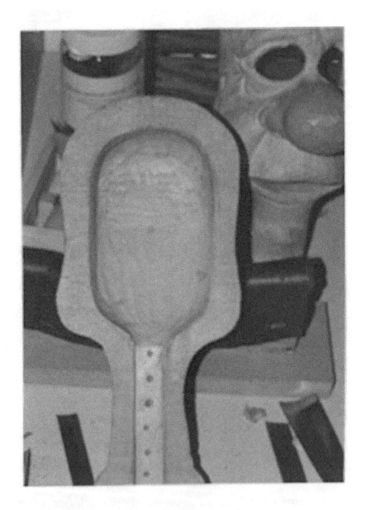

Back of head hollowed out and rough carved.

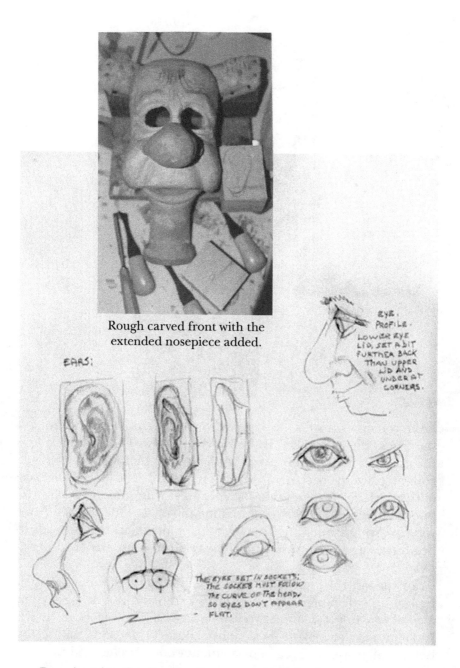

Rough carved front with the
extended nosepiece added.

EARS:

EYE.
PROFILE.
LOWER EYE
LID, SET A BIT
FURTHER BACK
THAN UPPER
LID AND
UNDER AT
CORNERS.

THE EYES SET IN SOCKETS:
THE SOCKETS MUST FOLLOW
THE CURVE OF THE HEAD,
SO EYES DON'T APPEAR
FLAT.

Drawing details of eye and ears, a reference for design ideas.

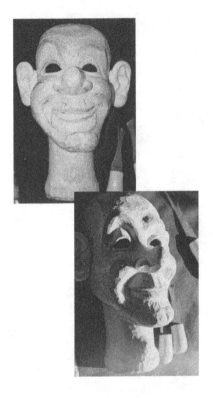

Next, you now transfer the drawing to your woodblock. The front of the block, the five inches, is the front face view. The six-inch side is the side view, and then the back of the head is on the five-inch back. You can trace the design or use carbon paper on the block. The base of the neck needs to be round like a ball as this is important for the smooth operation of the head turning in the shoulder socket. After you have transferred your drawing to the block, you are now ready to begin the carving process. The is the real fun—also the hard work.

I can suggest that you may want to sculpt from Plasticine a small replica of your design. This is an extra step and not necessary but a good way to get a look at your idea in a three-dimension model. You can make some revisions—longer nose, bigger eyes, and so on. Before you begin working in permanent wood, this method can save you some time in the end.

Rough-Cutting the Head

Head block with drawing of front profile. Side view with rough cutting done.

If you have access to a band saw that can handle this size of wood, then you will save some time. If not, then you will cut the facial planes with a handsaw. Place your work piece on the bench stop. To stabilize the bench stop, clamp it down to the work bench. Begin by cutting the side profile, and then go to the front profile. You will need to redraw the views after you have the side cuts made. Redraw your center line on the front view. Do not cut right up to the guide lines. You only want to remove the bulk, and the closer cuts are done with your chisels and rasp files.

Finishing the Carved Head

Once you have roughed out with the saw cuts, you now proceed with the chisel work. Begin your carving at the forehead and work your way down the face. Be sure to leave enough material for the nose. If you find that the nose you have decided on is larger than the material you have originally allowed, add a piece of wood for the nose. Glue and clamp an extra piece of wood to extend the material for the nose.

Use the large gouges and straight-edge chisels to work your way toward the final shape. The bench stop helps to stabilize the block on the bench. Push the tools by hand and with the carving mallet to remove the larger pieces of material. The wood rasp is very useful when shaping the round areas alternating between carving and filing.

Woodcarving requires careful measured cutting with your chisels. Always cut away from yourself and keep your hand away from the front of the chisel's path. When cutting away material, do not attempt to cut too large chunks, and be aware of the direction of the grain. Cutting against the grain can result in the splintering of large pieces, so go easy and take your time. Keep the edge of your tools sharp, touch them up with a smooth stone every now and then, and maintain your edge tools at their sharpest. Dull knives and chisels can be dangerous as they slip when you have to push too hard.

Keep checking your work in the mirror to see how your progress is going and redraw your guidelines and details as you work your way toward the final shape. When working the piece on your lap, be sure you have a leather apron or some heavy cloth to protect your legs from accidents.

The addition of a block for the large nose and, to the right of that, the eyes installed with controls.

In the beginning, you do not need to get too involved with details yet, but be sure to leave enough material for the eyes and ears. You can leave the ears off at this point if you choose and carve them separately after the head is completed (more on that later). The ears are attached to the front half of the head.

As you carve away more material to establish the main features, the large facial planes, the forehead, eye sockets, cheeks and jawlines, mouth, chin, and neck, keep in mind you need to leave enough material for the detailing.

Once you have defined these areas, redraw the eyes, nose, mouth, and center line of the face. You are now ready to go back over these features and work on the detailing. Next, do a mirror check for balance and symmetry, making sure you are maintaining the characters' features. Using your callipers, check your carving against the drawing. You want to be sure that you are staying within the dimensions on your plan.

Begin by carving the brow ridge, just above the eyes, and then start to define the eyes. The eyes are tricky; here, you need to go carefully and slowly. Using you callipers, measure the eye socket to conform to the size of the ping-pong ball, around one and a quarter inches. Carve the eyelids to the round shape of the eyeball. The upper eyelid extends slightly over the lower lid. Pay special attention to the corners where the upper and lower lids meet. The lower lid tucks under the upper lid a bit. This very fine detailing can come a bit later; for now, carve the eyeball shape, leaving material for the lids to be cut in. Keep in mind the size of the eyeball and its round shape; we do not want flat eyes. The outside corners of the eyes are set back a bit from the inside corners. This is what gives the round shape of the eye socket.

Next, start to define the bridge of the nose and work your way down to the nostrils. Redraw the nostrils and the area below the nose leading to the upper lip. The nose gives a lot of character to the face. It often defines the character type. I have always liked noses; as a result, many of my creations have larger-than-life noses. Noseworthy is an extreme example of a character nose.

Another thing: facial features on puppets are often exaggerated, the reason being they show up well onstage. Do not forget to carve inside the nostrils a little ways.

Moving on now to the cheeks and mouth, the cheeks are somewhat exaggerated, and you will have a crease line from the sides of the nose down to the corners of the mouth. If the character has a big smile, the cheeks will be bulged out and then slope sharply to the jaw and the tip of the chin. The mouth should be quite wide for good visibility. You want the audience to see the mouth open from a fair distance.

Head design plan.

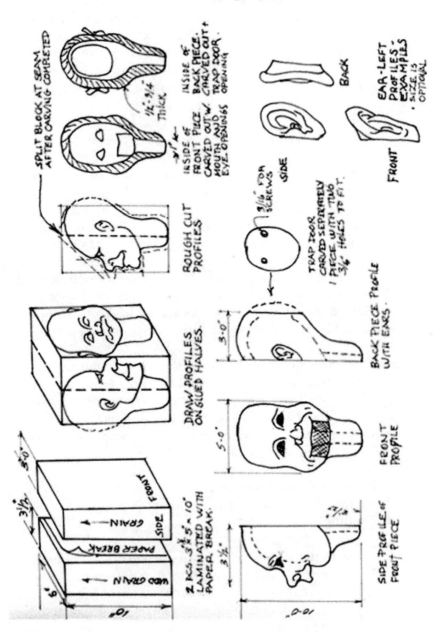

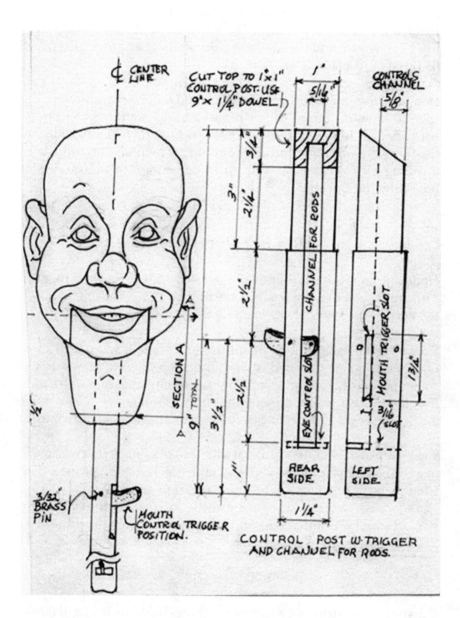

Design layout of head with control handle and mouth trigger.

The upper lip and curve of the mouth are important to get right. Once you have hollowed out the front of the head, cut the mouth out and a new one made with controls fitted; however, we will get into that later. You can carve in the jaw to complete the face. However, it will be removed, and the final one, with its mechanism attached, will be fitted in its place.

Don't try to complete the fine detailing and sanding at this point. You want to show all the features without the final finishing. We can go back after the head has been hollowed out, and then we can complete the fine work of smoothing and rounding. The final smoothing and finishing may become marked up while you are in the process of hollowing out the head.

Hollowing Out the Head

Hollowing out the two halves of the head is next on the program. This is a bit of a tough job, and you will have to go slowly to maintain the correct thickness of the head shell.

Start by prying apart the head at the glued seam. If you used a sheet of paper as I recommended in the lamination, the two halves should come apart easily. Carefully work your way around the seam with a wide flat chisel. Use a mallet, tapping the chisel as you go. Try not to mark or chip the edges at the joint. See drawing of head and mouth controls.

You have two halves. To begin, you will need to support the front piece in a large wood vice before you begin the hollowing-out process. The front of the face will have to be protected from damage while working on the inside. Before you begin cutting in, mark the perimeter of the sides, it should be about half an inch to three quarter inches thick. Refer to the figure;

Hollowing Out.

Use your power drill and a three-quarter-inch paddle bit. Drill inside of the marked line down to about a one-and-a-half-inch depth. From here, use you gouges to cut in deeper. At this point, with a quarter-inch paddle drill, push them through from the front of the centre of the eye openings down to about an inch and a half. This gives a guide to help locate the eye sockets when working in from the back. The thinnest tolerances of the head shell will be around the eyes. Use your callipers to check for thickness as you work your way in.

As you progress down into the head, it is important to know where you are in relation to the mouth opening. To help with locating the mouth, drill small guide holes from the front in the corners of the mouth. Use an eighth-inch drill, going down to about an inch and a half. Continue with working the inside. Smooth it out a bit with heavy sandpaper.

A tip for the eye sockets: glue strips of sandpaper crisscrossed on a wooden ball, the same size as the eyes. Rotate the sanding ball into the sockets. This is a perfect sanding block for the eyes. To help work with the sanding balls, I attach a large eye screw, providing a finger grip handle.

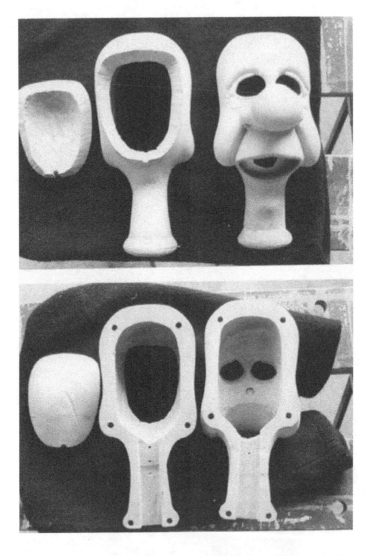

Three components of the finished carved head without the jaw, ears, or control handle. Holes drilled for dowels to assemble the head front and back.

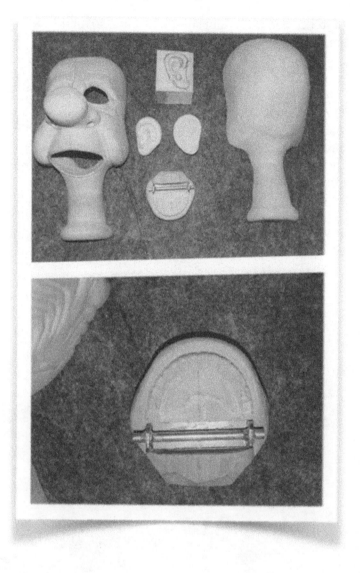

Finished head components and detail of the jaw with brass-
tube attachment for mouth axle. A brass hinge plate with
one side removed can be used as the anchor axle guide.

Once you have the head hollowed out, cut down the neck using your
handsaw and remove the material with a flat chisel. This will be the
slot for the head stick. Check the width of the head stick (cut a one-
inch square at the top and three inches down). Be sure that you have

a tight fit in the neck. The slot should be cut one inch wide. One half of the head stick will fit in the front and the other half in the back.

When cutting the opening for the jaw, the sides need to be shaped in an arc. This arc will correspond to the arc of the mouth axle or pivot point. This is a tricky job and will take a bit of time to get it right. You can gauge from where the pin for the mouth will be located—that is your center, and from there, you scribe an arc from the upper corner of the mouth to the bottom corner. When cutting out the mouth, follow these lines. These will determine the proper line of movement when the jaw opens and closes. The idea is not to have any projection of the jaw when it is in the open position; this can be a bit difficult to perfect. When fitting the jaw, the pivot/axle can be adjusted to meet the proper arc required.

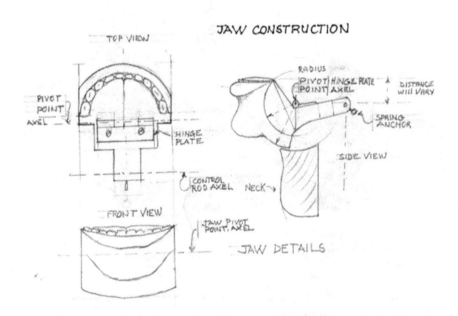

Jaw design

Jaw and control installation layout with rod and trigger. The eye control rod is shown below the jaw trigger. All controls and the control rod are installed in the front section of the head.

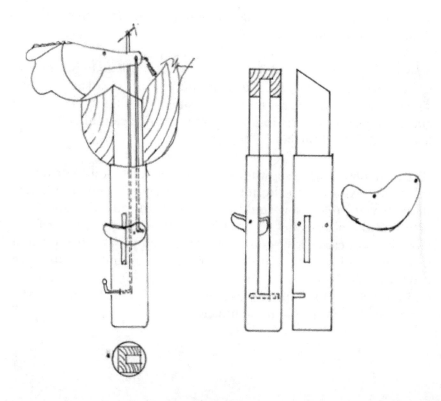

From the front, mark with a sharp chisel the outline of the mouth and carefully cut away the jaw from the front. Work in from the front and back until you break through. Try to be neat when cutting the sides of the jaw slot. Make the cuts on both sides parallel and as smooth as you can. This is important for the mouth movement. I make these cuts with a flat chisel and knives rather than a saw blade. See figure Mouth and Eyes Openings.

Back of the Head

Next, hollow out the back part of the head using the same technique as used for the front. You will not go as deep, so go carefully. You now have to fashion a separate piece for the trap door. Carve this to finish out the head shape as per your drawing. Remember, when carving the back of the head, cut a slot for the head stick in the neck as mentioned earlier. The back piece will have the ears carved into it or carved separately and attached later. Do not attach the ears until you have finished with the hollowing-out process. They may become damaged in the process.

Now that you have hollowed the head, we are ready to build the jaw. Check the mouth opening to be sure the sides are clean and square. The bottom line of the jaw at the neck should be slightly curved and cut at a slope down to the inside. You want a nice clean thin edge here for a good fit with the jaw.

If you are planning to show upper teeth, you may want to deal with those now. As a rule, I do not install upper teeth; only the lowers show. If you prefer, you could carve the teeth into the upper lip or install them separately. You only need to show four upper front teeth in most cases. I have used old dentures I pick up from dental mechanics offices; they have extra bits lying around, and they are usually available quite reasonably. The uppers look best if they are set into sockets. Building the jaw from a piece of bass is best. Cut the jaw out slightly larger than the finished size.

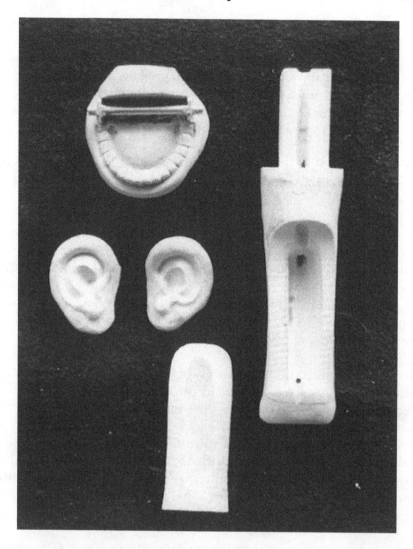

Lay out the jaw design on the block. The profile will have to have the arc inscribed on the side. This arc will have to match the arc you have on the jaw opening, worked out with a compass on paper, and then transferred to the carving. For the underside of the jaw, just below the chin, you have a small crease and a double chin. This will also have to have the same arc as the sides. Therefore, when the mouth opens, the jaw rotates down without gaps. You will do the fine fitting once the jaw axle is set, and you can work the mouth up and down to get a smooth action without sticking. You can use wood putty to fill as you need once you begin the fitting process.

Carve the teeth and tongue, or you may fit dentures down. I have found fitting a complete denture plate awkward; it is better to set each single tooth glued down and the back filled with wood putty. Before you can mount the axle, install the hinge plate. This is made from one half of one-and-a-half-inch brass hinge. Remove the pin and use the half with the two holes. The hinge is mounted on top of the jaw; this provides a solid adjustable mount for the axle.

Once you have the jaw cut and carved and fitted, you can now set in the axle. Use a brass rod, stiff enough that it won't bend easily. Do not use coat-hanger wire, too soft and not thick enough.

With the jaw in the mouth, set the hinge on top of the jaw. Do not screw it down permanently. Leave some room for adjustment, and this will give you the location of the holes you need to drill for the rod. Drilling the axle holes in the cheeks needs to be as accurate as possible. You can purchase an extra-long drill bit called a "bell hanger" drill bit. This will be approximately ten inches long and needs to be the same diameter as the axle rod.

Set the head into the large woodworking vice—this should have wooden jaws—and lock it in, careful not to damage the carving. You will need to block the neck slot so it will not collapse while you have the head mounted in the vice. Drill the axle hole with a power drill. If your power drill has a spirit level, that will help keep the drill bit level. This process is difficult, aligning the holes straight; however, do the best you can. You may have to re-drill and fill any mistakes, but that is how it goes. This process is a trial-and-error effort.

Once the hole is through both sides of the cheeks, line up the hinge on the axle, Mark the location of the hinge screw holes. Adjustment will need to be made to the hinge placement, so do not attach the hinge permanently; set it in place with pushpins while you are aligning the axle. Once you have the jaw working smoothly on the axle, you can screw down the hinge plate.

With the jaw working smoothly, remove the pin and attach the mount for the spring as shown in the illustration. Use an eye screw and drill a hole for the rod that moves the mouth. This hole should be a good fit for the mouth rod without any free play. Refer to the detailed drawing of the mouth mechanism.

Refit the jaw with the axle. Do not permanently fix the axle yet. You will be fitting and refitting when you install the control rod and handle. The sides of the jaw or slots of the mouth must fit very closely. The better the fit, the better the illusion of reality. Besides, we want to do a good job. If the slots or gaps are becoming too wide after you have finally fitted the mouth and it works smoothly, you can backfill these gaps with plastic wood putty. The way you do this is you use a narrow strip of brass sheet and work it in and out of the gaps with the putty. The same goes for the gap at the bottom of the jaw, at the neckline. Fill and sand until you get a close seam.

This whole process is time consuming and detailed work. If there is one feature on the figure that counts for the success of the animation, it is the mouth movement. It should be as closely fitted, as smooth operating, and as accurate as you can make it.

Examples of jaw design on two different characters.

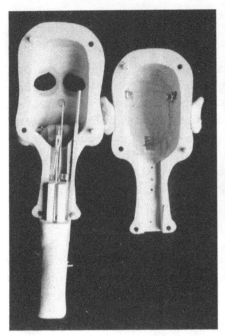 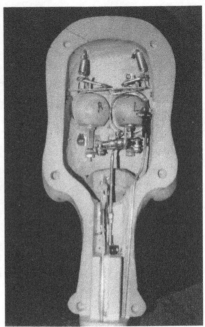

Front and back of head shown with head stick and control rods for eyes and mouth. The back of the head shows the trap door attached.

Upper right shows eye controls installed; right side shows head with head stick and trigger for the mouth.

This is a detailed look at the two halves of the head front and back and ready for the jaw, eyes, and control handle.

The handle is cut from a dowel, usually curtain-rod material, one inch or one and a quarter inches in diameter. I prefer to carve the head stick (handle) separately and give it a bit of shape to fit comfortably in the hand, be it right- or left-hand control. Check to determine which size is more comfortable for your hands. The smaller size dowel is best for head movement, allowing more room to maneuver. Use a solid hardwood, beech or birch, for the handle; it wears better and is more rigid when drilling control mounts and slots, does not splinter, and provides a good finish as unfinished wood.

Painting the stick isn't recommended. I prefer to use unfinished wood. Alternately, you can wrap the handle with a fine chamois.

This absorbs hand perspiration and gives a nice feel to the grip. The overall length is nine and a half inches, with a three-sixteenths-inch-wide slot cut down the back. The holes are drilled for the mouth-control lever and the eye-rod control, located below the mouth lever. Refer to the drawing for dimensions and layout.

Cut at the top of the three inches of the handle an approximately one-inch square to fit into the neck slot. The placement of the mouth lever depends on whether you are operating the puppet—with your right or left hand. Activate the lever using your thumb; thus, the control lever goes on the left side of the handle for a right-handed operation and on the right side for left-handed. This is determined from the front view of the head. See the illustration for layout.

Cut along the length of the control rod, giving two halves. The grooves for the mouth and eye rods are cut into both side halves. The cut is a quarter inch wide and runs a quarter inch deep on both halves and runs along the inside of the handle from the top to within one inch of the handle bottom (see illustration for details). Cut slots for the mouth trigger and eye-rod button as shown.

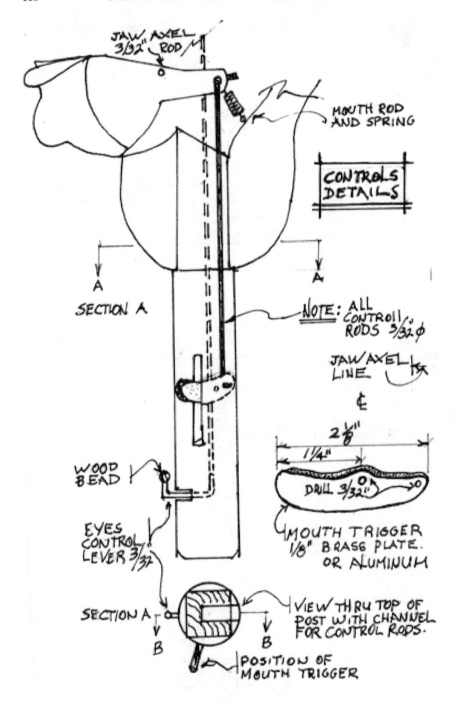

JAW AXEL
3/32" ROD

MOUTH ROD
AND SPRING

CONTROLS
DETAILS

SECTION A

↓ A

NOTE: ALL
CONTROL
RODS 3/32 ϕ

JAW AXEL
LINE

₵

2 1/8"

1 1/4"

DRILL 3/32"

MOUTH TRIGGER
1/8" BRASS PLATE.
OR ALUMINUM

WOOD
BEAD

EYES
CONTROL
LEVER 3/32

SECTION A

↓
B

↓
B

VIEW THRU TOP OF
POST WITH CHANNEL
FOR CONTROL RODS.

POSITION OF
MOUTH TRIGGER

Remember that the thumb operates the mouth trigger; position it on the *side* of the control stick. Position the eye-control button on the *front* of the handle two inches below the mouth trigger, operated by the fourth or fifth finger.

Cut the control lever for the mouth from a thick piece of brass and drill two eighth-inch holes for the axle pin and for the push rod. When installing the lever in the handle, it must fit without any side play; the fit should be very close with no room for rattling. Use small brass washers to take up the slack. What you want is very smooth operation. WD-40 is a good lubricant for this area. Cut the axle pin from a piece of brass rod the same diameter as used for the control rod.

Cut the brass push rod for the mouth, measuring the correct length from the trigger to the back of the jaw, allowing extra length for the bend that goes into the trigger and jaw. Insert a brass bushing for the control-rod connection at the trigger point. This helps to prevent wear and makes for smoother operation. Install the mouth and attach the control rod and trigger. Test the mouth movement with the mechanism for smooth and noiseless operation. Install the return spring on the jaw as shown in the illustration. This process of fitting the jaw and trigger will take trial and error to get just right.

Once you have everything working correctly and a smooth noiseless operation of the mouth, without any sticking points, you can anchor the mouth-trigger pins with epoxy glue and fill in with wood putty and smooth with sandpaper. When fitting the control handle into the neck, be sure the slot that carries the control rod that moves the jaw is aligned below the lowest point at the back of the jaw. Next step, we need to assemble the eye movement and controls.

Eye control layout showing placement ideas for springs. The spring located in the bottom diagram is the best placement.

The eyes are made up from either ping-pong balls or wooden balls. The size is dependent on the character, as I mentioned earlier, during the face-carving stage. I recommend that the ping-pong ball diameter, one and a quarter inches, is a good standard. I have also found excellent eyes glass and acrylic on-line. There are a few companies that provide eyes for dolls, and museum displays and are high quality at a reasonable price. Go to glass/acrylic eyes in your browser and a number of options will appear. This is a new discovery for me and I recommend looking into this. The eyes are available in standard and larger sized, I like to use 28mm or 29mm size, larger than most human eyes. Use acrylic, these are easier to work with when drilling and mounting.

Cutting the opening for the iris is tricky in the case of the ping-pong balls; use an electric Dremel (rotary cutting tool). You can also cut by hand with small curved manicure scissors. In wood, cut a depression in the ball so that the iris fits flush. A tip on marking and cutting an accurate depression is to find a piece of tubing with the same diameter as the iris, file the edge sharp, use it as a scribe to cut the circle in the ball, and then finish off with the Dremel tool, creating the depression.

Drill axle holes for the vertical axles as shown in the figure drawing. Using a sleeve around the axle's top and bottom so that the eye is locked on centre and rotating freely. Attach an L screw to the back of the wooden ball or to the axle sleeve (see figure 13) post inside the ping-pong ball. Set them temporarily into the eye sockets. If they do not rotate smoothly, remove and sand down with the eye-socket ball until the eye rotates freely without sticking. Be careful not to overwork the socket as it will become larger than the eyeball.

Once the eyes are set with the iris and working smoothly on the axles, remove and paint them with glossy white enamel. Two or three coats should do. Check the tolerance of the eyes in the sockets; you may have to re-sand the sockets slightly to fit the eyes in the head, so be sure they still rotate smoothly without sticking. The paint will have altered the diameter of the eye, so be careful to allow a bit of space for clearance, allowing the eyes to move without rubbing on the lids.

The alignment and placement of the eye axles is a fiddly and precise job. In some cases, I have used strips of leather for the upper eyelids, which can be painted and then fitted and glued in. This is a good remedy for eye sockets that are too large for a close fit. The leather is good looking, and it can lightly touch the top of the eyeball and give a smooth appearance of a close fit. If the eye is not rotating perfectly smoothly, the leather gives a little and allows for too large an eye opening or a slightly protruding iris. I used this method on Noseworthy, and it looks very natural. Paint the eyelids. Oils work well on leather.

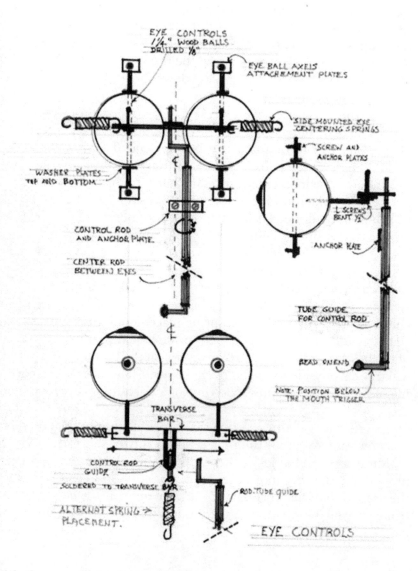

EYE CONTROLS
1/4" WOOD BALLS
DRILLED 1/8"

EYE BALL AXELS
ATTACHEMENT PLATES

SIDE MOUNTED EYE
CENTERING SPRINGS

SCREW AND
ANCHOR PLATES

WASHER PLATES
TOP AND BOTTOM

L SCREWS
BENT 1/2"

CONTROL ROD
AND ANCHOR PLATE

ANCHOR PLATE

CENTER ROD
BETWEEN EYES

TUBE GUIDE
FOR CONTROL ROD

BEAD ON END

NOTE: POSITION BELOW
THE MOUTH TRIGGER

TRANSVERSE
BAR

CONTROL ROD
GUIDE

SOLDERED TO TRANSVERSE BAR

ROD TUBE GUIDE

ALTERNAT SPRING
PLACEMENT.

EYE CONTROLS

With the eyes set in the head, centre them and measure the distance
between the L screws in the backs of the eyes. Cut a piece of brass plate
as shown in the diagram called the transverse plate. Drill the holes
for the L screws and mounting points for the return springs. Next,
bend a piece of wire and solder one end to the centre of the plate as
shown. The length of this loop will have to adjust by trial and error so
that the control rod travels smoothly along its length without binding
or stopping before its complete cycle. The way to do this is to solder
one end of the loop, bend it to the estimated length once you have it

working, and then solder the other end. The loop of the wire must fit very closely to the eye-control rod that comes up from the handle. If the loop is too wide, the mechanism will be noisy when operated. I insert a piece of rubber tubing over the rod where it goes through the loop to help keep the clicking noise down during operation.

Refer to the illustration for details on mounting the transverse plate and spring attachments. Install the control rod as shown into a brass-tube guide before bending the bottom end first, insert the rod, and determine the bending points for the upper section that travels through the eye-loop extension. This refers to the control-rod guide loop that is soldered to the transverse bar. Refer to the eye-control drawing. You will need a needlepoint set of pliers for this. This is a fiddly bit of business. There is some trial and error to get it just right.

You may have to try different mounting points for the springs to get the exact amount of clearance for the transverse bar movement and centering of the eyes. The springs should be very light and short and cut to size if needed. The best spring placement for the eyes is in the centre of the transverse plate, one spring attached at the back inside of the head. The finger-control extension at the bottom of the handle will travel from side to side, moving the eyes. The slot for this control may need to be lengthened, allowing for a full range of eye movement.

Once you have all this working, along with the mouth movement, it is now time to set all the pins permanently in the handle for the mouth trigger and axle for the jaw. Use epoxy glues and fill in with putty if necessary; smooth over. Now we move on to the next stage: the control handle. Permanently attach the control handle to the front part of the head, as I mentioned earlier, screwed down and glued in place.

Attaching the Back Section of the Head

With all mechanics installed, permanently attach the back to the front half. The two surfaces need to be very smooth and flat, fitting together without any gaps. For added stability, insert wooden dowels. Dowel drill sets with guides and dowels are available for this process and make for accurate drilling and matching of the dowel holes.

Fit the two halves together with wood glue and clamp. If you can find one, use a flexible strap clamp, designed for clamping rounded and odd-shaped work pieces. Otherwise, large wooden-jawed woodworking clamps with rubber protectors will work.

The Ears and Attachment

Now that you have the head together, sanded and the filled the seams and completed the fine sanding of the head, the ears have to be created. If you have not carved the ears as part of the head, you will have to carve and attach them as separate pieces.

Ears are very interesting facial features; they can define a character. As a rule of thumb, ears are sized by measuring the distance from the eyebrows to the bottom of the nose. This is a general guide. Lower-placed ears, sticking-out ears, small ears, large ears—all give the character a different look and will enhance a type, be it older, goofy, young, etc.

Experiment with clay models before you get into carving the ears. Experiment with different sizes and placement on the head. I have drawn a typical ear for you as a guide. You can be as detailed as you want or carve them with simple lines, suggesting the ear lobes, curves, etc. It can be challenging trying to get them perfect. I tend to like this kind of detail work and spend a bit of time working them out. Once completed, attach them with small screws through the inner ear, glue, fill, and sand to perfection.

Next, attach the trap door. Cut a shell shaped to the back of the head as shown with two holes drilled for mounting. Hollow out the trap door, making it as light as possible, and screw into place with countersunk holes.

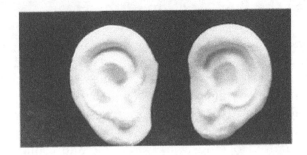

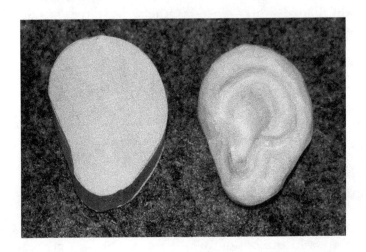

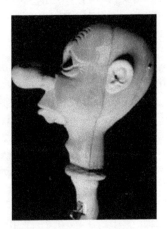

Ears attachment on the back portion of
the head. Carving the Hands

Hands are a challenging project. Drawing hands is difficult enough, let alone carving them. If you want to maintain realism in your character, details are important, and hands play a big part of the character's realism. I have seen figures built with hands that look like either featureless stuffed gloves or claws. I believe we can do better than that, so let's try it.

Carving hands is a project in itself, but with patience and perseverance, you should be able to create a decent pair of hands. You can be very detailed with nails, creases, and all the fine features, or you can carve the shape and suggest the detailing by painting it in. So long as the shape of the hand is correct, the hand will look good.

Alternately, for a simplified version, you can use the cartoon-character hand, the kind you see on Disney characters. You will notice that these hands are missing one finger. You will see a thumb and three digits, very simplified without creases or fingernails, and usually, they are white gloved. This is the classic cartoon design. I am not so sure if that is what we want here, but it is your decision. This type of hand is effective on, say, a Pinocchio puppet, for example. However, this is not recommended for the more real-to-life characters, as in the more traditional ventriloquist's figure, which is where I am going here.

The overall size is important. Small hands look like doll's hands, and large hands tend to look like they belong on another figure. A rule of "thumb" for sizing the hand to the puppet: cup you hand over your nose with the bottom heel on your chin, and the tips of the fingers should come to the eyebrows. Apply this method to your character's face, measuring from the chin to the eyebrows. This is a good general rule and allows for a naturally cupped hand. If in doubt, I tend to build the hands a bit larger on male figures and smaller and more slender for female figures. The index finger can be pointing a bit if you like, but to make things easier for your carving, keep the fingers aligned together. Make the hand cupped a little, about the same as when you placed it over your face for sizing the hands.

Carved hands tend to be fragile when they dangle from the figure's sides or packed into the suitcase. The fingers will break. So be thoughtful of this when carving delicate or separated fingers. As a guide for lifelike hands, you can use your hand as a model; art and anatomy books are good references. Draw the design as best you can from top and side views and transfer this design to your wood piece. When drawing the hands, look at the different views: top, sides, and inside. Note the relationship of the fingers—which ones are longer and thicker and how and where the thumb connects. Look at the fingernails and draw them in, or you can just paint them on. For realism, I cut in the nails with the Dremel tool or by hand and then work the nails with jeweller's files. I have carved hands that are shaped to hold objects; in one instance, I had my character holding a cigar or a Coke bottle.

Hands are tricky to draw well without any special features, such as shaping fingers to hold objects. I advise you keep it simple. Spend some time to get the basic shape right. You need to remember an obvious detail: be sure to draw the right and left hand. Do not do what I did in the beginning: start to carve the second hand from the same pattern. You could end up with two right or two left hands. This is obvious but worth mentioning. The hands show character as well as age and gender. A female hand differs from a man's hand, which is usually heavier and wider with thicker fingers. A woman's hand will have more refined, longer, and usually painted nails. Children's hands are, of course, smaller and have a definite look of youth. An old person's hands tend to be boney with large knuckles and have veins showing, often discoloured. When designing your character's hands, keep these factors in mind. You would be surprised how often I get comments on my puppet's hands. People do notice details, and as I have said before, details add to the overall reality and interest of the character.

Once you are satisfied with your design, transfer it to the block and begin the rough cutting of the main planes of the hands. Cut by hand or on the band saw.

If you are going to use jewelry, like rings, you need to consider this when shaping the hands. Round out the top of the fingers so that a ring sits naturally. I usually buy cheap costume jewelry rings, cut out a bottom section, and glue it on with epoxy on top of the finger. Do not try to slip a ring on over a finger. It is not worth all the effort, carving the fingers separated, and makes the finger more fragile.

You also need to consider the overall size of the hand and thickness of the wrist. If they are too large, you will have problems buttoning shirts and fitting jackets over the hand. There is another option for wardrobe considerations. I have designed my characters' hands so that they are removable from the arms. This is handy if you intend to have a variety of wardrobe changes. I also remove the hands when packing the dolls for travel. When flying, I pack the head and hands separately in a carry-on bag.

Paint the hands with the paint you used for the head. Coat the fingernails with clear nail polish; this adds a nice touch of realism. Apply a clear coat of flat non-shiny spray lacquer over the entire hand; this protects the finish and makes for easier cleaning and removal of scuff marks.

The photo shows the final finished left hand with slots for the nuts, which are mounted in recessed pockets, drilled with a screw nut to take the control rod. The rod is threaded to fit in the inserted nut. I like the arm rod around ten to twelve inches in length. Experiment and see what suits you. The longer the rod, the less visible your arm and hand. The rod needs to be removable to allow for clothing changes on the figure, assuming you have different costumes for the character.

Animation

I prefer to use removable arm-control rods rather than fixed, but that is optional. I use one rod on the figure's left arm as I am right handed operating the head, so my left hand does all the arm movements.

I notice many vents move the puppet arm by just lifting it and waving it around—not a good look, in my opinion. The rod provides a much nicer illusion of the figure's independence and detaches you from the obvious operation of "assisting" the character like he has a paralyzed arm. The arm-rod length varies, the longer the rod, the less visible your hand as it stays down below your waist. Use wrist movement as much a possible so as to keep your arm action minimal. I like to use the puppet's arm for gestures, but don't overwork it; a little movement in the right places works effectively.

Animation features like moving eyebrows and arm-rod operation, I use sparingly. You can get carried away with the constant action of a movement feature, and I believe it becomes a distraction. The ones that I use more other than the mouth, of course, are the eyes. They follow the head movement; with the left turn of the head, the eyes follow, for example. Also, the eyes show different moods and attitudes along with the head. Arm gestures are good for emphasis of what is being said by the character. It is a good idea to sit in front of a mirror and practice different expressions and synchronized movements to create an attitude or add emphasis to what the puppet is saying.

Just remember—when you are speaking, make sure the character doesn't look "dead." Animation and movement is critical to maintain the illusion of "life" in the puppet. He/it is always aware and listening or somehow reacting to what is going on around him.

I knew a performer who had a very nice subtle movement for his character. It sat on his knee, and one or both his legs were moving, swinging back and forth every now and then. Great effect.

Body Design and Construction

The clothes determine the size of the puppet body. I use children's size, 6X, in most cases. You will still have to make some modifications to the sleeve and trouser lengths. This makes it easier to buy clothing off the rack and gives you more options when choosing your partner's wardrobe. You can have custom-made clothing if you wish, but bear in mind that this can be almost as expensive as the equivalent of adult custom tailoring. This option of custom tailoring is obvious when you are creating a special outfit, like a uniform, a clown costume, a chef outfit, a sports uniform, etc. I call this "themed costuming."

Getting back to the "body building," the body construction method I use is heavy compared to some. I create figures that are sturdy and built to last. Consider your characters will probably outlive you, so build them to withstand a lot of handling, packing, and travel. You also want it to be reliable; we do not want an arm or leg falling off during a performance, which has actually happened to me. This disaster is just too funny and embarrassing for words.

The Body Frame

The shoulder plate is an important part of the figure's body. The shoulders give the proper shape for the clothes, and whole body-frame construction hangs on the shoulder plate. Use basswood for the shoulder (dimension: eleven by three and a half by two and a half inches). You can laminate two pieces together for the required thickness.

Begin by first scribing with the compass a two-and-half-inch diameter hole for the neck. After drilling a starter hole, cut with a narrow hole saw or coping saw blade.

As a guide for the slope of the shoulder's angle, I use the common coat hanger as a guide. It has the correct natural shoulder shape. Lay out the shoulder on the wood and cut with the band saw or by hand, carefully following the dimensions in the drawing. Carve the shoulders sloping down from the back to the front, narrower at the shoulder ends (refer to drawing for proper shape). Leave a vertical bevel edge around the front and sides of the shoulder plate, approximately half a foot flat, for the slots to attach the rib ends. Once the overall shape is established, carve the neck opening so it forms the bottom half of a socket, shaped to fit the bottom of the neck, providing the ball and socket fit we are looking for. Finish off the socket surface, lining it with a soft leather cover. Glue down with contact cement.

Carve a depression on the underside of the shoulder plate, reducing the thickness, allowing more room for the hand when manipulating the head (refer to section Drawing Detail of Shoulder Plate, page 190). Finish off the top and underside by sanding, making the surface smooth, especially the underside. This is where all the action will be with your hand operating the head. You want the underside surface smooth—no splinters to scrape your knuckles. You could also lay in leather on the underside of the shoulder plate, a backstop for your hand.

This is one example of a body construction, very simplified. The ribs are cut from yellow cedar. The hands are stapled to the arm tubes on the inside and attached to the shoulder with staples. The length of the arms is somewhat shorter than in a natural human body proportion. It looks better and keeps the arms in a more natural position and out of the way. I like to attach a wire from the shoulder down to the hands inside the arm. This allows for bending the arm slightly at the elbow, more useful on the puppet's right arm. The left arm doesn't need a wire, allowing for movement with the arm rod. I like to use copper wire for the wired arm. Did I mention you need pillow-stuffing material for the arms and legs? Craft shop for this.

Torso Design with Curved Ribs

This is a light construction. Cover the frame with canvas stapled on.

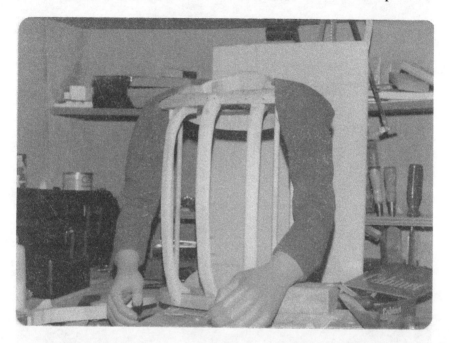

The wood used in this example is yellow cedar. Also, pine or basswood works well if you don't want to use a harder wood. The base can be five-by-eight 3/8" inch plywood.

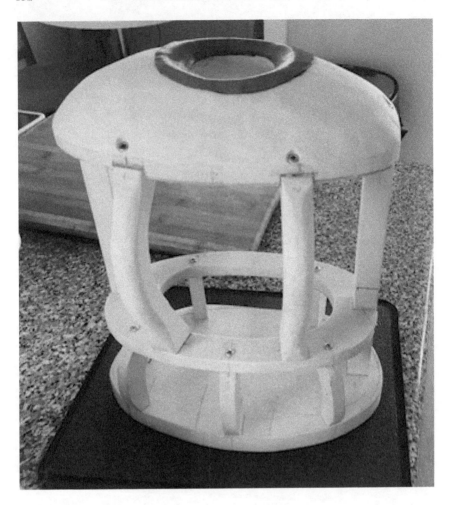

The body frame shown here is for a female character.
However, the basic rib design would be flatter or bulge
at the bottom for a thicker belly form. The frames vary
as you can see; it depends on the character design.

Shoulder Plate (go to page 139)

The bottom plate shape should match the shoulder plate curve; do
this by tracing the outline of the top onto the piece for the bottom.
The bottom plate width is an inch shorter than the top. Cut the
bottom plate as shown in the drawing. This will be flat on both sides
with the edges sanded smooth. The ribs will be recessed into the
top and bottom of these plates. The rib slots need to line up the top

and bottom. Place the base under the top plate and scribe the slot markings through both pieces. Cut the slots as shown in the drawing. The slots need to line up perfectly so that the ribs fit top to bottom without bending.

The ribs should be cut from a hard wood, either oak, maple, or beech; these woods are strong and won't split when screwed to the top and bottom plates. Use the pattern designs as shown in the diagram. For the ribs, band-saw or hand-cut the ribs, sand and pre drill the screw holes, and countersink the holes in the ribs so that the screw heads are flush with the surface. The shoulders protrude beyond the torso by an inch; this gives a more natural fit for the arms and allowing underarm room for the jacket or shirts to appear more natural when draped over the torso. As a final finishing touch to the torso, I recommend spray-painting the interior of the body with a flat black paint. This helps conceal the interior of the figure when you are working the doll. I have found that on occasion, I have to turn the figure around, showing the hand entering the body.

Once you have the body together, the frame has to be covered with a canvas material of medium weight, the same material artists use for painting. Measure and cut the canvas, allowing a little extra for folding the edges for stapling to the frame. If you want a bit more softness and shaping to the torso, you can apply a thin sheet of Poly-foam under the canvas to build it out. If the figure is a female, you may need to add some extra foam material to build up the bust. This can be cut from thicker foam to give the proper form. The same applies if the character is heavyset or has a potbelly.

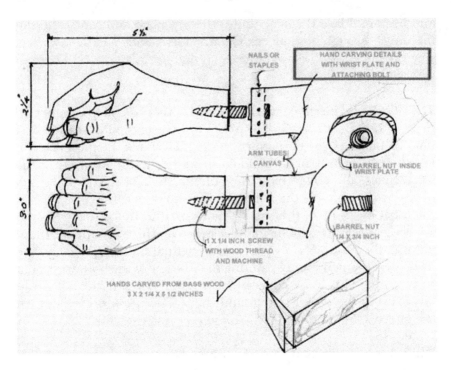

The mounting screw with bolt end is what I use to remove hands from the body for travel. You needn't do this. More easily, the hands are stapled to the fabric arms as shown in the previous photos. I have created removable hands for packing and travel. Wood hands are fragile and fracture easily. As a precaution, I cover the hands with a sock when the figure is stored or traveling in a case.

Cut the arms and legs from the same material as the body covering. Cut the tubes for the arms as shown in the figure's arms and legs. Stitching the canvas pieces together on a sewing machine is best. You may hand-stitch, but it is hard work when sewing canvas. After the sewing is complete, turn the tube inside out so the seams are inside. Stuff the arms and legs with fibrefill material, available in craft shops. For a better shape of the legs, I insert a piece of light plywood, one eighth inch thick and approximately two inches wide, for the underside of the upper part of the thighs. This gives a more stable sitting of the torso and defines the knees. You will notice that the length of arms and legs appear to be short for the figure. This is done on purpose. The figure looks more compact and natural with shorter limbs. This also makes it easier to position the doll when sitting. You want the legs to stay put in a position without flopping around with the feet turned in different directions. Attach the hands and feet to the arms and legs before attaching to the body.

Once you have the arm and leg tubes stuffed with hands and feet attached, attach the arms to the shoulders by drilling four holes through the shoulder plates, using shoelaces to attach the arms. You can staple them if you prefer. Staple the hands to the ends of the arms. If you are using the removable system for the hands, do this now. Be sure to leave a half-inch unstuffed flat section of canvas above the hand to allow for natural wrist movement.

I recommend cutting recesses under the base plate for the leg attachment. This leaves the base of the body flat without any surface protrusions, which tends to make the doll body unstable for sitting; you want a perfectly flat surface. Attach the legs to the body underside with a strip of leather over the canvas and then screw down into the recesses. Alternately, you may attach the legs to the top side of the bottom plate or on the underside. Either way is workable.

Before starting to carve the feet, purchase the shoes first. Carve the foot to fit the shoe. It is easier this way, and then you know that the foot will fit the shoe you have on hand. I have used children's size 8 to 9 in most cases. The feet are carved from basswood as shown in the figure drawing. Cut from one solid piece or laminate two sections to give you the height. Keep in mind that the foot will be rigid, of course, so you will find that an exact shoe-sized foot will be difficult to fit. Allow some space for fitting by making the foot shorter, and use lace-up shoes if possible; these are easier to fit on a rigid foot form. Finish off the foot by sanding and apply a coat of flat clear acrylic paint. This makes it easier to fit socks and shoes and preserves the wood. Attach the feet to the leg tubes using three-eighth-inch staples.

You have completed the body, all arms and legs in the right place, left hand on the left side, feet in the right place. Okay, I know you knew that, but I have made dumb mistakes with hands on backward and feet on the wrong side, so it is a good policy to always check your handiwork. Now let's move on.

Place the head in the body and test for smooth operation. Be sure there is enough clearance under the shoulder plate for easy head manipulation. Attach the arm rod on the left hand as described earlier; check the illustration for this detail. I use a ten-inch threaded aluminum rod, about three sixteenths of an inch in diameter, threaded into a barrel nut, set into to the wrist section of the hand. The rod needs to be removable to allow for the puppet's wardrobe changes. Wrap the rod with black non reflective tape or spray-paint with a flat black.

Standing Legs: Optional Design

I have mentioned my idea of standing legs. This feature adds a fair bit of weight to the body and also poses a problem for packing the doll into a standard-sized suitcase. I use thirty-inch cases, pretty much the standard, but the figure with the head in stands close to forty-two inches. I pack the head in a separate case whenever I travel. This ensures the head is protected, especially with air travel, which I do a lot of these days. I have debated about including some details about this style of leg design. If you want to tackle this, I have laid out plans for your information if you want to incorporate that feature into your character. As I mentioned, it does add weight to the figure and poses problems with packing.

I have found black PVC plumbing tubing, two inches in diameter, works well. The tricky part is attaching the tubes to the body with a solid axle at the hips and one for the knee. I have worked with wooden leg designs similar to what you might see on a marionette puppet. This makes for even more weight, however, and is not the best choice, in my opinion.

Cut the tubes for upper and lower legs (top/thigh: seven inches long; lower leg: six inches long) and then insert a knee-joint riser, two inches long, into the end of the top of the lower part of the leg. Be sure to put a couple of screws to hold them in place. Drill a three-sixteenths-inch-diameter hole for the axle through the riser and leg tube. For the knee to lock in standing position, screw in place another two-and-a-quarter-by-one-inch length of PVC tube over the top of the top part of the lower leg tube.

On the bottom of the body plate, attach a wooden anchor block, one and a half by one and a half by five inches long, to hold the upper/thigh axle and then drill a quarter-inch hole from end to end of the anchor bar for the single axle of three-sixteenths threaded bar. This is inserted into a brass tube for smooth rotation. The threaded bar is available in random foot lengths from a hardware store. You have to cut it to nine three-quarter-inch pieces in length to create the hip joint. I push this axle through a brass tube for smooth rotation and leave enough thread on the ends to lock them off with locking nuts. Once you have the legs positioned at the hip but not permanently attached, work on the knee joint.

Note: In a sitting position, the legs are forward, sitting on the bottom of the body plate. This tends to make the figure unstable and tip backward, so you have to place a seat block at the rear so the bottom of the body behind the leg assembly creates a secure sitting posture.

The joint at the knee requires a one-inch-diameter dowel in the lower leg with a one-and-a-half-inch vertical flat projection cut to allow the knee to bend. Alternately, you can use a piece of flat wood stock shaped to fit in the leg tube. Drill through the tubing and wood knee projection to take a threaded axle, which is set through brass tubing, and the axle is locked off on both ends, or you can use a bolt with a locking nut on one end.

Once the legs are attached, you have to stabilize the figure with rubber-band tubing on the back legs. You have to adjust the rubber-tubing tension to balance the figure, not too taut so that the figure can still be seated but tight enough to give some balance to the figure when it is standing when you are working with it on a table stand. If you hold up the body from the floor, the legs should hang backward a little with the tension of the tubing. When standing, the legs are in a neutral position, so when you bend it forward when standing on the table, the tension on the rubber tubing will keep control of the body from tipping too far back or forward.

I have also created a type of "knee cap" rubber band that keeps the legs straight and stops the legs from collapsing at the knees when standing. I have found this tubing in medical supply outlets. It is similar to the exercise rubber bands, tubes you find at workout equipment supply stores. The bands come in several different sizes and tensions, sometimes referred to as surgical tubing. You can use exercise bands in red or blue, which seem to have the right tension. There is some trial and error when working with the different tensions to get the right effect. Attaching the rubber bands can be tricky. I have drilled holes into the leg tubes and inserted the rubber tubing, tying a knot to hold them in place.

The feet, assuming they are carved wood, need to be mounted the same way with a bolt through a brass tube at the ankle. I use a short strip of rubber tubing to create a rear tendon that holds the foot in a down-forward position. This makes for better balance when standing and keeps the feet flat on the table. A tip: set the feet slightly off, pointing out, not straight ahead. It looks more natural and provides a better balance if the doll is standing. I sometimes add a small piece of Velcro to the soles of the shoes and a rubber mat on the performance table so the feet don't slide around when you are working with the figure. If the figure is wearing sneakers, this won't be a problem as they provide enough traction usually to keep the feet in position.

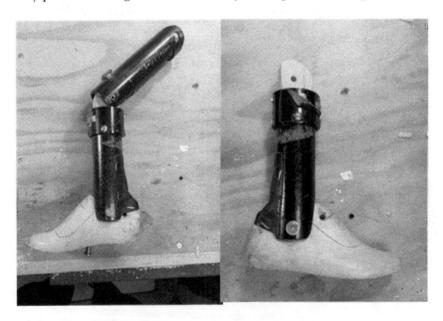

This completes the building project. Now you have to think about the costume or, if you like, wardrobe for the character. Of course, this is entirely up to your own idea of what/who you started out to create. Young, old, middle-aged, male, female, etc. The clothes define the character and help make the puppet more real and give it personality.

The puppet should be looking pretty good by now. You have the head painted, hair on, and the body assembled and ready for clothes, costumes, whatever you decide. There are many options.

Shoulder plate with opening and lower-body base plate.

I have seen great children's clothes in department stores and goodwill stores—lots of options. If you are having a costume made, then be prepared for an expensive wardrobe. If your character has a pirate or soldier uniform, for example, you may find something in a Disney shop. I notice that around Halloween, there are a good number of shops that sell kids' costumes of all kinds. If it is a boy character, that is the easiest to find. There're lots of trendy outfits for kids.

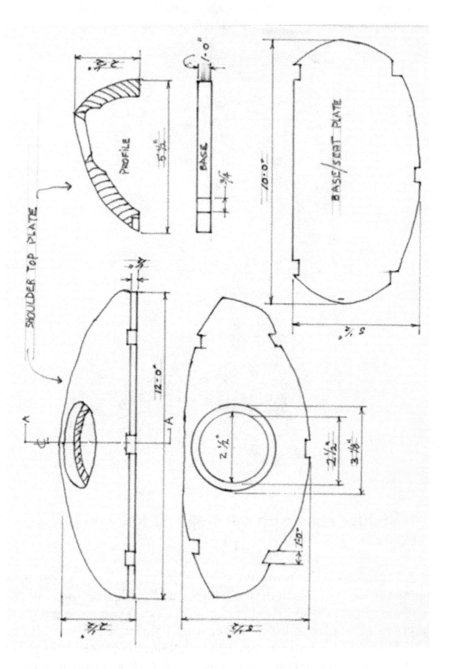

Cover is stapled to the torso using a medium-weight canvas, same type used by artists for painting, also same type for the arms and legs.

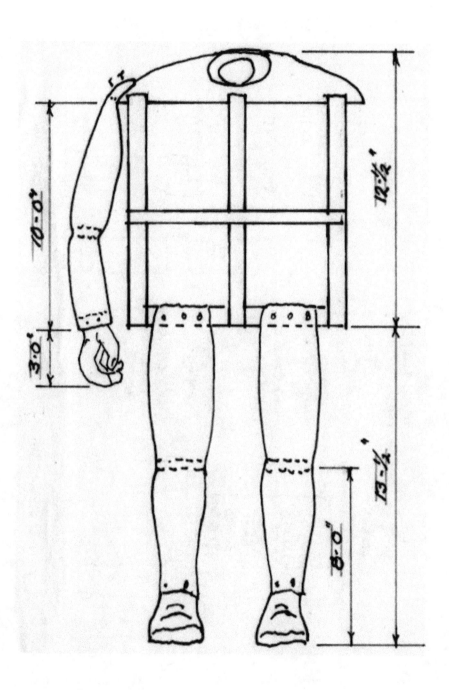

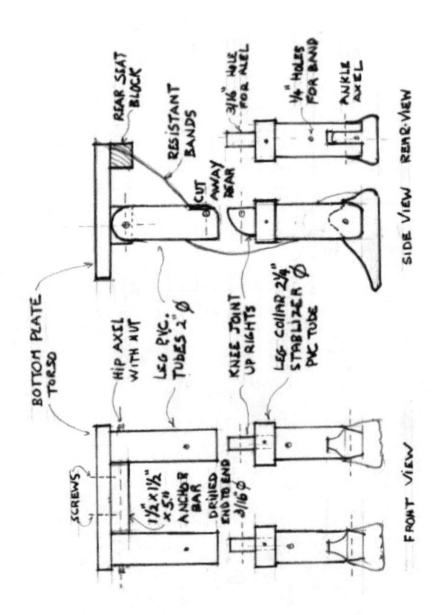

REAR SEAT BLOCK

RESISTANT BANDS

CUT AWAY REAR

3/16" HOLE FOR ALEL

1/8" HOLES FOR BAND

ANKLE AXEL

SIDE VIEW   REAR VIEW

BOTTOM PLATE TORSO

HIP AXEL WITH NUT

LEG PVC. TUBES 2" Ø

KNEE JOINT UP RIGHTS

LEG COLLAR 2¼" STABILIZER Ø PVC TUBE

SCREWS

1½" x 1½" x 5" ANCHOR BAR

DRILLED END TO END 3/16 Ø

FRONT VIEW

Based on my sizing of the figure's body, you should find sizes 6 to a 6X a pretty close fit. You may have to have the legs and arms of shirts or jackets shortened as the puppet leg and arm lengths are purposely designed shorter than normal human proportions. Shoes again depend on the foot size you created, probably a 9 in kid's size, but don't make them too small. Feet always look better a bit larger, I think. Also, if the figure is on standing legs, larger is better.

A set of legs I had on Noseworthy, same design as shown in the drawing. The feet were antique shoe "lasts," used for building children's shoes, perfect shape but very heavy. I use rubber-tube bands for the springing, attached below the knee and to the front of the base plate or to the top of the knee on the upper part of the legs, and another set of bands from behind at the bottom of the top leg segment and attached to the back of the base plate. Refer to drawing (page 195). The bands need to be adjusted so the legs are under tension but remain in a straight standing/neutral position. You will have to adjust the balance with the head in the body to get the right weight distribution. This arrangement is really a great way to give the character an independent attitude.

Some examples of different costuming ideas. I often theme my characters to match the event I am working.

Dressing the Figure

After you have completed the body and all painting, place the head in the body and check to see that the figure sits firmly and upright on a chair or table and everything looks and works perfectly. As an added security for the head, I attach a piece of elastic to the bottom of the head stick and loop it into a hook in the base of the body. This ensures that the head does not fall out of the body when handling the figure—it does happen.

When dressing your partner, keep in mind details. If you have to have the arms and legs shortened on the clothes, have it done professionally. It will look so much better and give the character a more convincing personality. Whichever way you choose for wardrobe, give thought to what you are putting on. Study character types that resemble your partner's type. Use coordinated style and colors. Alternatively, consider the complete opposite. Whichever you decide, it will add or take away from your character's personality and believability. Remember, details make for the whole effect.

Once completed and you work with your creation, getting to know all about him/her/it, you can refine your material and ideas about the personality. I would suggest you write a biography of the character. Where is he from? Who were his parents? What are the pet peeves? What are the likes and dislikes? The more you know, the better. As you work with the figure, you may find that you will make adjustments.

You should be proud of your work, and now you can begin the process of developing your character and your puppet's relationship to you. You as well as the puppet have a role to play, and this will develop as you go along. You will have lots of fun. Your character will end up being a part of the family (in a good way). Send me a photo of your creation. My website is Donbryan.com. From there, you can follow up with an e-mail.

Chapter Six

Animation

We will now move on to the next area of practice, and that is animation and control of the figure, which bring your character to life. There are basic rules to remember when performing with a puppet, and these rules are important to remember when creating the believability of your partner and instilling it with a personality all its own. This personality should be totally opposite to yours, which goes without saying; if not opposite, then different. This means a different voice, attitude, gestures, timing and pacing of dialogue, and habits of speaking where words or phrases typical to that character are in the dialogue. The exception to this is if you have created a "mini-me," a miniature of yourself. That presents a completely new concept, requiring a study of your personality, creating a characterization of yourself, focusing on your personality traits, and then exaggerating them to be bigger than life. This becomes a project of self-analysis.

Getting back to the topic of animation, always maintain the life in the character. Remember he/she sees, hears, thinks, responds, and moves. You want to keep the life illusion continuous, not just to the audience but also to yourself when you are performing. I do not recommend getting so involved with the character that you start having arguments with him in your room after a show. Treat the puppet as if it were a real person when on stage. Do not continue the illusion beyond the performance, unless you are rehearsing with it.

I know vents who talk about their puppets as if they were real people in their lives, not just putting us on but really believing it. That is going a bit too far, in my opinion, bordering on weird or bizarre behaviour. I mention this because I have seen it happen, and this can become a fixation with some people. Remember it is a puppet, and you need to be aware of the fact; you have control of all that it says. Strange advice, maybe, but there are some folks who, for whatever reason, use their characters as a stand-in for an alter ego or a friend they imagine or, even worse, a member of the family. I suppose if you were to talk to a psychoanalyst, he might have a name for the problem, and I bet it is difficult to spell.

Ventriloquist dolls are quite simple as the bodies are hollow, the arms and legs stuffed tubes, so their range of movement is limited. You can use the rod puppet technique whereby a rod is attached to the arm or the wrist of the arm nearest you. This simple and effective bit adds life to the body. The other arm is anchored, so it does not swing around "willy-nilly." This tends to look like the character is a stroke victim. One method of anchoring the arm is using a piece of wire looped around the thumb and hooked in the top of the trousers or belt, keeping the arm from swinging around. The same goes for the legs; be sure the feet are both pointing forward in a natural manner and have some definition, showing a knee joint. This looks so much better than a limp rag doll leg, hanging like a "boneless chicken leg." Do you get the idea?

Most vent dolls today, especially custom-made figures, tend to have a variety of movement built into the heads. These are great for effect and bring the character to life, provided you do not overuse all these effects continuously. You use the effects as an accent to what is being said or heard, not as a feature in itself. It is easy to get carried away with overworking the animation. This can distract from the performance and keep you busy fiddling with the controls and not concentrating on the performance. This is where I believe that saying "Less is more."

Edgar Bergen characters were the simplest—head and mouth movement only. Yet he managed to bring his puppets to life very convincingly—and on radio yet! Paul Winchell and, later on, the Muppets, working on television, were able to utilize many more animation techniques. When you consider that on television, the performer is up close and personal with his audience. This is a much more intimate show. The audience can appreciate the use of effects, such as eyes, eyebrows, upper lip movement, and other innovations.

To help you with your animation, I recommend sitting in front of a mirror with your character, having a rehearsal conversation, and trying different head attitudes and eye movements as the character talks and listens. I think it is a good idea to pay attention to people engaged in a conversation. Notice where the person is looking when they are speaking and listening. Watch how people react to one another during a conversation. The listener may be nodding in agreement or shaking their head in disagreement. Looking sideways at the speaker registers suspicion. You can create emotions without actually speaking but by using body language. Experiment in front of the mirror.

One habit I have noticed some vents have is their tendency to have to always look at the puppet when it is talking. That becomes distracting to your audience and tends to focus too much on "how you are doing." You do not need to monitor every move of the character. Look away and make eye contact with your audience. Keep them in the picture. You can register expression on your face to what the character might be saying. Do this while the puppet is talking. This is more effective than your face looking out with a wide grin on it during the whole time the puppet is talking. Some vents use this method of lip control, using a tight smile whenever the puppet is speaking, and it looks strange and unnatural. People don't smile all the time when talking to one another.

On the puppet's mouth synchronization—I believe I mentioned it earlier, but I will again—when the puppet speaks, the mouth movement should open with each syllable and at different tempos. I have seen some acts open the doll mouth once for a multiple syllable word. For example, *fantastic*—that word has three movements, "fan-tas-tic." Do you get the idea?

If your character has moving eyes, they should move in the same direction the head turns. Observe people as they look around to speak to someone. Their eyes look in the direction that their heads are turning.

Gestures and movements are derived from the character's personality. If your guy is hyperactive, an extreme type, the movements will show the speedy nature or the reverse if the character is laid back and less interested. Consider these as traits when building your character's profile and biography. If your puppet is a senior person with slow responses, less-than-perfect hearing, and memory lapses, this too adds to the development of material and is reflected in the animation of the character.

When I was at the convention, I was able to look in on several acts as they performed in the amateur showcase. I was impressed with the skill and variety of some of the performers. However, there was a performer who seemed to have a lot to say himself and few lines for the character. This in itself was not as entertaining as hearing what the character was saying in response to the straight man, the vent. The other distraction was while the vent was speaking, he left the character lifeless, just hanging there until it was his turn to speak—not a good thing. You need to keep the character animated during your lines or, at the very least, make it look like he is paying attention or not by appearing distracted, maybe doing some bit of business, looking around, being bored, or some reaction of some kind, not just being lifeless. Remember, the audience wants to believe the puppet is a person, and it is your job to bring it to life and maintain that illusion.

To Sit or Stand?

Having the puppet sit on your knee is the most common way of working the act, and you can either sit or stand with your foot up on a chair. This is the better of the two methods from experience. Standing rather than sitting gives a much better visual to the audience. You will show up a lot better in most venues as people in the back of the room can see you and the puppet. Sitting on a chair or stool is very traditional and was used extensively by early vents, but the disadvantage is you are too low on the stage.

Another method is to sit the puppet on a small computer stand, the type that is collapsible and will extend high enough for you to work off of. This way, you have more freedom of movement, and the character is not so connected to you, presenting a more independent appearance for your partner. However, you do lose the ability to move the figure's body back and forth with your knee/leg action. This does help keep the puppet movement going and does enhance certain "attitudes" the character may adopt. One disadvantage of the figure on your lap while you have a leg up on a chair is your lower back may start to give you a problem. I suffered from a pinched nerve in my left leg and circulation issues because of having my leg up on a chair for extended periods. That may be an issue only common to me for various physiological reasons, but it is worth noting the potential for problems. That is why now I always work my act with the puppets either sitting or standing on their tables.

There are no set rules for how you present you act. You may sit with puppet on your knee, the old traditional pose, or your leg up on a chair as I mentioned above. The preferred method today seems to be the character sitting on a small high stand table, with the vent standing. The magic shops usually have tables that are good for this. There are small portable computer tables available.

I have one from a company called In-stand. I am not sure if they are still available, but there are others you can locate online. Noseworthy stands on his own legs on one of these tables, a nice independent appearance that separates you from the character and gives you more mobility. In addition, the character can have some body movements that are not available if it is sitting. If you have a rod on the puppet's left arm for movement, it is easily animated when the character is standing.

I created a design for standing legs many years ago. I am surprised that more vents haven't adopted standing legs. It does create a problem for suitcase packing. The doll has ridged legs with articulated hip, knee, and ankle joints that are spring-loaded, so the character is always balanced when standing. You still have to support him, but the overall look is excellent and separates you from the figure. The art of performing with a "knee" figure is the traditional approach and is the style that I pass on to you.

Being a traditionalist in my presentation style, I have explored other possibilities here in this book. However, keep in mind the options are endless for creative input from yourself. Often rules are broken or modified to suit one's ideas. You are allowed to think "out of the box or out of the suitcase," as it were. Today innovation is often the key to originality. This is how we progress and become pioneers in our chosen professions. Do not be afraid to fail. That is how we learn.

Bergen once said, "Success comes when preparation meets opportunity." In other words, know your craft, perfect it, rehearse it, and be ready. The opportunities will come. With today's technology, you can experiment with anything you can imagine.

I have continued to be very traditional in my approach. However, I have taken advantage of some electronics and mechanical devices to enhance my performance. No matter what you experiment with or create with a view of being original, always maintain a high standard of perfection. Learn the basics and learn them well. Once you have mastered the fundamentals of your craft, you can innovate, improvise, and extemporize whatever you decide. You will build on your foundation of solid technique. After performing hundreds of shows in all varieties of venues and experiences will you then become a seasoned performer, a true professional.

I have been performing in front of live audiences since I was a kid for over sixty years. I still learn something new, and it never ceases to amaze me that I still have new revelations. The unpredictability of performance art, audiences, venues, and events demand your flexibility and challenge your ability to adapt. The process never ends. You are a student of your craft. Be the best you can, enjoy what you do, and perform like you don't need the money. Watch your dreams and creations unfold before you, amateur or professional, and be sure to have fun along the way.

Carving your own character is a challenge, as I said. Don't be discouraged. It will be a project that will take patience and time. Remember—no matter how many mistakes you make or how slow your progress, you will still be way ahead of those who didn't even try.

My DVD is available on my website, Donbryan.com.

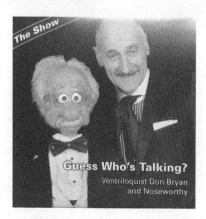

In Conclusion

So there we are then. That covers it, I hope. So much of what I have written here is from my experience of working as a professional performer for more than forty-five years. Building puppet characters has not been my main pursuit, but the craft, with its challenges, continues to fascinate me. I love working at it, trying new ideas, trying new innovations and mechanics, always trying to perfect my next creation, making it more interesting and unique if possible.

I build mainly for myself and have not taken on a commission for many years. That is not to say I would never build commercially. Having said that, I do the odd one now and again. I find I am too busy working as a performer to spend a lot of time in the shop. It does have its appeal for me as a retirement project, but I am now over seventy-five and not thinking about retirement yet. I am too busy enjoying my career as a ventriloquist, making people laugh and enjoying the whole illusion of bringing my characters to life. I love what I do, and I hope to still be at it for a few more years.

As I said, I don't consider myself a figure builder in the sense that I am promoting myself for commissions. I do it more out of the enjoyment and the creative experience. There are several really talented figure makers who are far ahead of me in this rarefied field of ventriloquial figure building. I put more emphasis on the enjoyment of the process, not so much on the volume and production of commercial puppets. I am a traditionalist and enjoy working in wood. This takes more time and has its artsy appeal for me. I have tried other materials and find I much prefer working with wood, a natural material that appeals to me, shall I say, in an organic way.

I hope you enjoyed the book, I had fun writing it, and now that it is done, I am thinking about my next project. I need to have a project on the go. We never stop learning and creating. I love the process. I hope the instructions were complete enough. My next project will be a video of puppet building—sounds like a must-do now.

Good luck with your new character. Drop me a line and let me know how it worked out, and I would love to see a picture of your creation. Best of luck!

www.donbryan.com

Yours truly,

Don Gaylord Bryan

Autobiography

Don Bryan lives in North Vancouver, British Columbia, Canada, and still performs regularly in the cruise-ship market and corporate events, traveling throughout North America with his sidekick Noseworthy and family. He is considered to be one of the foremost performers in the art of ventriloquism and the figure-building craft, a lifelong pursuit of perfection and dedication to the art form. His vocal technique and skill is highly regarded among his peers.

In this book, Don shares his secrets of ventriloquism and his figure-building expertise that he has developed over the past five decades. This book is also a tribute to his artistic mentor, Mr. A. M. "Pop" Steinman, who set him on his early path to the artistry and his lifelong passion of figure building, and also to the legendary ventriloquist of yesteryear, Mr. Edgar Bergen, who became his friend and mentor, encouraged Don during his earliest years, and, to this day, remains an inspiration.

This book will present the imperatives on learning the art of ventriloquism, the technique, practice lessons, and a comprehensive look at the performing aspects of the working ventriloquist. This book is intended to not only coach and teach the novice and enthusiast of ventriloquism but also serve as a guide and refresher course for working performers, with tips on how to improve the act, to help create an original presentation, and to develop inspired ideas, with the goal of expanding on the traditional presentation of the ventriloquist's art. For those of you who are already in the business as a professional, there are ideas and information on everything, from technique, writing, and the development of material to the character creation, puppet animation, stagecraft, and performance tips.

"Don Bryan is certainly one of the most respected and entertaining ventriloquists of our generation. This book takes you on a journey of his life as well as sharing his secrets to being a great ventriloquist and for anybody interested in building your own figure this is worth it's weight in gold."

Acknowledgment from Paul Romhany (Performer, Author, and Editor of Vanish Magazine a monthly magician's publication.)

CPSIA information can be obtained
at www.ICGtesting.com
Printed in the USA
LVHW04s0453280818
588324LV00001B/6/P